When the Vow Breaks 2:

Pain & Forgiveness

Twins Write 2 | Lakisha Johnson

Gratitude

I'm going to always start by thanking God because without Him, I am nothing! God has given me an amazing gift, that I shall never take for granted.

I'm grateful to my husband, children, family and friends who are often ignored when I'm writing.

To my sister, Laquisha, Shakendria and Tia for helping me with feedback on this series. You ladies rock!

And to YOU, who continually support me ... THANK YOU! I could not do this without your support! Please don't stop. Keep reading, reviewing and recommending!

Dedication

This book is dedicated to you. Thank you for taking the time to support me. You don't have too and because you do, I appreciate you!

When the Vow Breaks 2:

Pain & Forgiveness

When the vow breaks, tears will surely fall, but will the marriages survive the damage of it all?

Chapter 1

Ray

Justin and I pull up to the house, at the same time. I get out and grab my things, taking my time to walk in, behind him.

"Ray, what the hell was that? How long have you been sleeping with your boss?" he screams.

I look at him and roll my eyes.

"Answer me! How long?"

I lay my things down on the counter, close my eyes for a second and take a breath. Then I walk over and stop a few steps from his face.

"Shorter than the time you've been sleeping with yours."

His face looks like the blood is being drained out as he stumbles back.

"Is that your shocked or I didn't think you knew, face? Which one?"

"How— "

"How did I find out?" I interrupt. "Glad you

asked. See, when I was in Gatlinburg," I grab my phone, "I got this, from your boo." I open my videos and press play, turning the phone around to allow him to see himself, down on his knees. "This is you, isn't it, dear husband? The one giving sloppy toppy to a man?"

"Ray— "

"Save it Justin and get the hell out of my house."

"No," he yells causing me to turn around. "Let me explain."

"Nigga, who the fuc—"

"Why are y'all yelling?" Rashida, our daughter asks, coming into the kitchen.

Justin and I both turn to look at her.

"Well, you want to tell her, or shall I?" I question.

"Tell me what?"

"Ray, don't, not yet," Justin begs.

"Rashida, your dad and I are getting a divorce."

"You're kidding right?"

"No and although I planned to tell y'all, in a

much better way, it's happening. Very soon."

"This is so messed up," she says.

"I understand but right now, I need to finish talking to him." I point to Justin.

"Rashida, until we've had a chance to talk to your brothers, please don't tell them." Justin requests.

She rolls her eyes, "whatever."

"Ray, that was foul," Justin says as soon as she leaves. "You could have, at least, waited until we were done talking."

"No, what's foul is the fact my husband, of sixteen years, is gay. What you should be thankful for, is me not telling her that."

"Ray, please."

"Ray, please," I mock. "I can't believe I didn't see the signs. You haven't touched me, in months and although I'm grateful now, I should have known. Hell, your dic—"

"I get it, please stop," he says as if I'm getting on his nerves.

"Why should I? Were you telling Travis to stop

when he was shoving his penis in your mouth or when he bent you over? We're you yelling stop, so you could be honest with your wife? Were you telling him to stop when you thought about how this would affect our children?"

"Ray, please, I'm sorry. I didn't mean for this to happen, but you've been cheating too."

"Oh, no boo-boo kitty, you are not about to flip this back on me. I cheated because I hadn't had sex in months, with my husband. You though, you can't say the same because I've been offering myself to you. You didn't want it because I wasn't what you wanted.

And, yes, you meant for this to happen because a penis doesn't just slip into your booty or mouth. God," I chuckle, "the least you could have done was be the top."

"Ray, if you would just let me explain."

"You don't have to explain shit to me, but you will need to figure out a way to tell your children. Oh, and find somewhere else to stay." I grab my keys and walk out.

Getting to the car, my phone rings and it scares me. I press the button, on the steering wheel.

"Hello," I answer with a pissed off attitude.

"Ray, this is Thomas."

"What's up Thomas?"

"There's been an accident and Cam is in the hospital. I've been trying to call Shelby, but she won't answer."

"Is she okay? Where is she?" I question.

"Regional One and I just got here and don't have a lot of details but it's bad."

"Okay, I'll get in touch with Shelby and we'll be there."

"Please hurry," he hangs up.

Lyn

I pick up my glass water bottle, throw it against the wall and scream. I'm pacing in my office when my phone rings. It's Paul, I decline, and he calls again.

"What do you want?"

"Lyn, please give me a chance to explain. Please."

"Go ahead."

"Uh," he stutters. "Can we do it face to face at the therapy appointment and I'll explain everything?"

"No, talk now!"

"I can't because Kandis is threatening to take my son and I need—"

"Wow," I chuckle. "You know what, fuck you Paul!"

"Lyn—" I disconnect the call.

A few minutes later, the back-doorbell rings. I stomp to the door and push it open.

"GET THE HE—oh, I'm sorry. I thought you were

someone else. Xavier, what are you doing here?"

"Whoa, Ma. Are you okay?"

"No, but I will be," I tell him wiping the tears.

"I can help you with that," he smiles.

"Xavier, I am not in the mood and I'm not your Ma, so please leave."

"Wait," he says stepping inside, "it looks like you could use a friend." When the door closes, he moves closer to me. "I don't know what or who has upset you, but I can fix it."

When he wipes the tears from my cheek, I snatch him by his shirt and kiss him. He turns and presses my back against the wall. He's working to undo his pants while slipping his tongue into my mouth.

"No, stop," I pant. "This isn't right."

"It doesn't have to be right, as long as it feels right."

He moves to kiss me again, but I stop him.

"I'm sorry Xavier but I never should have kissed you. I'm upset, right now and not thinking straight. This cannot happen between us and I'm sorry I allowed you to think it would."

He stands there looking at me.

"You're a tease and you can't keep playing with people's emotions."

"I'm not playing with your emotions but you're a child and I'm married."

"It's cool." He turns towards the door.

"I'm sorry—" before I can finish, he turns back and punches me in the face.

"Bitch, today you're going to be more than sorry." He pulls a knife from his pocket and presses it against my neck. "Turn around, lift that dress and remove your panties."

I slowly begin to turn but when he steps back, I punch him in the face and run towards the door. He grabs me by the hair.

"Damn," he breathes, "for a big bitch, you sure can move but you aren't fast enough."

"Don't do this. Let me go and I won't say anything. Please."

He twists my hair in his hand, causing me to cry out.

"Please stop!"

"Now you beg," he laughs. "I'll stop when you quit fighting because I'm getting what I came here for. Next time, you'll stop being a tease and you'll think twice before trying to get me fired."

I'm down on my knees, crying and pleading. He spins me around.

"Lay down and shut up," he orders.

He presses his knee into my back and uses his other hand to raise my dress and cutting my panties off. He's still holding my hair and it feels like it's being pulled from the roots.

"Okay, I won't fight but please stop pulling my hair."

He releases it, grabs me by my chin, pulling my head back and pressing the knife against my neck. "If you move, I'll split your throat and just in case you think I'm playing." He slides the knife along the side of my neck; I cry out and he laughs.

"The next cut will be deeper."

He stands up, kicks my legs open and I hear him unzip his pants. I silently cringe before praying. Getting on his knees, he grabs my hips to pull me to him.

He leans over, licking my ear before he enters me. His hand goes around my neck and with each pump, he squeezes harder. Blood is falling on the floor under me.

"Damn, I knew this was going to be good," he breathes into my ear.

After a few minutes, I feel the knife drop, down by my right hand so I moan a little and he sits back. He removes his hand from my neck to bring me closer to him as his speed increases.

"Yea, I know you want it. Give it to big daddy."

I raise up on my hands, turning to look at him, out the corner of my eye. When I see his eyes close and his voice change, I slide the knife under me.

"Ah," he grunts, slapping my butt over and over.

"I may have to get this again. Ah, yea, how'd you like that big baby?" he taunts.

Tears are spilling down my face and when he slaps me again, I grab the knife and swing it, connecting with the side of his neck.

He falls back on the floor and I jump up, hitting the panic button on the alarm panel.

A few minutes later, the door flies open, and Paul comes rushing in.

"Oh my God, Lyn."

"No, don't touch me," I scream pushing my back against the wall and pulling my dress down over my knees.

I close my eyes and sob while he calls the police. Minutes later, they come rushing in, with guns drawn.

"Ma'am, can you hear me?" one of the officers ask. "Ma'am?"

I nod.

"We have an ambulance on the way, stay with me."

I nod, again.

"Sir, I'm going to need you to step out."

"I'm not going anywhere. That's my wife and she need me." Paul yells.

"I understand but this is an active crime scene. Please step out and I'm not asking."

Shelby

"That night, when I left this house, I went to a bar where I sat trying to figure out what the hell had just happened. I didn't understand why I was being belittled and called names, by my husband.

A husband who vowed to love and cherish me. A husband, who vowed to never go to bed angry. I didn't get why you'd intentionally treat me like that. You called me a whore, a liar and a cheater."

"Shelby, what does this have to do with what we're talking about now?"

"EVERYTHING!" I yell. "While at the bar, I met a guy. I was so angry and hurt and since you'd already accused me of cheating I—"

"Shelby, please tell me you didn't sleep with this man," Brian cuts me off.

I open my mouth, but nothing comes out.

"Shelby, please," he begs.

I run into the bathroom and slam the door, pressing my back against it while sliding to the floor.

"Oh God," I cry. "Why couldn't he have been cheating?"

"Shelby, answer me," Brian screams while beating on the bathroom door.

I stay there, I don't know how long. After not hearing Brian, I open the door to find him pacing in the bedroom. I take a deep breath and begin speaking before he even notices me standing there.

"I was so hurt and confused that when a man, I'd never met before, left his hotel card for me at the bar, I almost used it. I was so angry that I almost did something stupid, with a man I knew nothing about."

"Shelby, I—"

"No Brian," I angrily say. "You don't get to console me when you made me feel so worthless and small. Sure, it would have been stupid of me, to sleep with that man but I wasn't thinking clearly. Although I knew I'd done nothing wrong, your words hurt me enough to not even care about my own wellbeing. And now, to know this, makes it so much worse. I'm the one you're supposed to confide in. ME!"

He closes the space between us by grabbing my arms and pulling me into him. I sob into his chest before I begin to hit him.

"Shelby, please just listen to me," he says, pinning my arms. "There were so many things going on in my head that I didn't know what to do. "I'm sorry."

I pull away from him. "You're only sorry because you know I didn't sleep with that man." I say with anger piercing my voice. "Would you be this forgiving, if I had?" I ask as my cellphone rings.

"I didn't mean for things to go this far and I, absolutely, did not mean the things I said to you. It's just, I never thought that I would be diagnosed with brain cancer."

"And I did? Do you honestly think that's the first thing that came to mind? Hell no! My first thought was cheating and man, I wish you had. Brian, you were wrong to keep this from me."

"I wasn't thinking and I'm sorry."

"Sorry doesn't fix this and it doesn't erase how you made me feel. You really hurt me."

He opens his mouth to speak but my phone rings, again. I snatch it from the nightstand and see that it's Thomas, I press decline.

"I know baby and I'll spend every day getting you to forgive me. Yes—"

My phone rings again. I press decline.

"Yes, I know I handled this the wrong way but right now, I need you."

My phone rings again, this time it's Ray.

"Ray, can I—Ray calm down. Your phone is breaking up. What did you say? Where is she? Okay, calm down and listen to me. I'm in the middle of something and cannot leave. I'll call Lyn, but can you please check on Cam and call me? I'll be there as soon as I can."

I hang up.

"Damn it!"

"Shelby, what's wrong?" Brian asks.

"Cam's been in an accident."

"Where is she?"

"Regional One, downtown," I reply walking in circles.

"Let's go. I'll take you to check on her."

"No, I'll go in a little bit but right now, we need to finish this."

"It can wait," he says.

"NO IT CANNOT!" I yell. "Brian, you just told me you have cancer. This shit can't wait because I've been waiting weeks, as is."

"I know, and I'll never be able to apologize enough for keeping this from you, but you've got to know that I didn't do so, with ill will."

I chuckle. "Whether it was ill intent or not, you should have told me, the moment the doctor thought something was wrong, other than migraines."

"I agree but I can't change that now. All I can do is ask for forgiveness and for you to be there for me."

"Just like that? You want me to forget the names

you called me, the hateful way you spoke and the nights you didn't come home? You want me to run into your arms and console you, while you deal with what you've known about for weeks?"

"Shelby—"

"Shelby, my ass. You were wrong for this. PERIOD! And just like you've had time to deal with this, now I need time. Stay with the baby and I'll be back, when I can."

I go into my closet and close the door. Leaning against the wall, I pull a shirt from the hanger and stuff it into my mouth, to stifle my scream.

Once I'm done, I close my eyes.

"God, please forgive me for coming to you when things are chaotic and not when they're calm, but I need you. Please Father, whatever has happened to Camille, let her be okay. You have the power to heal and whatever your will is, for her life, may it be done. And God, while you're sending a blessing to Cam, can you also give us strength, for this season of sickness, we're about to endure? Amen."

Kerri

"Kerri, I was stupid and childish. I didn't set out to ruin your dream, but I feared you changing."

"Changing?"

"Changing into an independent woman who wouldn't need me after all this," he says.

"What do you mean?" I ask, confused. "Everything I do, has always been for us. Michael, from the moment we met, we each had dreams, yet I put mine on hold while you went to school. After you graduated, with two degrees, you set a goal to make partner; so, I waited again. Then you made partner at the firm and I got pregnant with MJ."

I pause. "MJ is almost two and I'm at a place where it's finally time to do this, for me. I thought you'd be happy and supportive but instead, you walked out. When I needed you the most, you weren't there, and an apology doesn't erase that."

"Tell me what I can do."

"You can give me space."

"Kerri, please don't give up on us," he pleads.

"I didn't, you did."

"And I've said I'm sorry."

"Yeah and what am I supposed to do with your apology? It can't make up for the disrespect and the time you weren't here."

"I know but you can accept it, forgive me and let me make it right," he says coming closer to me. "We've both made mistakes so can't we just move pass this."

"Yea, you're right about moving pass this because I have. I've moved pass this marriage and you."

"That's not what I meant because I'm not letting you go," he asserts.

"Um, you can't hold on to something moving. Michael, I'm tired, for real and this back and forth I'm not doing. You relinquished the rights, to hold on to me, the moment you chose drinking and women, over your wife and son."

"Damn it, how many times do I have to apologize?" he screams, hitting the table. "I messed up, we're both aware of that but can't you forgive me? I'm willing to forgive you."

"Thank you but I don't need your forgiveness to sleep at night. Dude, you show up acting like this is easy as putting bleach on a stain and removing it. Sure, I slept with another man but that was after you'd walked out. It doesn't make it right, but I didn't put us in this situation, you did."

"I know," he huffs.

"Oh, well, do you know the man you turned into because I sure in hell don't? That man was not the one I married. Instead he was a completely different person and I'm having a hard time believing it was only because of the bakery. So, can you and he talk and find out in order for me to see if continuing this conversation is worth it?"

"Babe, the man sitting here is the one you

married. I want to go back to what we had."

"Nah, because going back means accepting the person you were, and I don't want him because he doesn't know how to deal with his issues."

My cell phone rings. I go over to get it and see that it's Ray. I press decline.

"Good because I don't want to be that person anymore. I'm —"

"Pause," I say when my phone rings again. "Ray, hey, can — wait, slow down. What hospital? I'm on my way. Yea, I'll call her."

"Let me guess, it's one of your girls."

"I'm pretty sure you heard me say Ray's name but yea and I need to go."

"Just like that, in the middle of our conversation? See, this is also part of the problem. Those damn girls can call, and you'll drop everything and run."

"That's a bold face lie. I've never put them, anybody or anything before my family. I've always been the doting wife, catering to your every need but right now, I'm doing me."

"Kerri, wait," he says grabbing my arm. "This isn't going how I planned. Can you please hear me out?"

"Look, I appreciate you coming here, to talk but it'll have to wait because Cam had an accident and I'm going to check on her. Am I walking out, in the middle of this conversation to do it? Yes, because those girls, were the ones who were here when you walked out. They helped me with my dream and I will not turn my back on them simply because you showed up to talk. Now, I need to get MJ and get to the hospital."

"I can stay with him," he says causing me to stop and look at him. "Kerri, he's my son and I won't hurt him."

"I'm not worried about you hurting him, but I am worried about you leaving him."

"I promise, I am not going anywhere. I'll stay with him."

"Michael, please don't make me regret this."

I grab my purse and head out, dialing Chloe's number.

Chloe

"Todd, wait. This is your baby."

He stops but doesn't turn around.

"I'm sorry I didn't tell you, but I didn't know how. It's not like there is a relationship between us."

"You're right so how can you be sure it's mine?" he questions, turning to face me.

"I don't sleep around, if that's what you're insinuating. Yes, I know I slept with you, the first night we met but I'm not usually like that. Besides my husband, you're the only other person I've been with."

"Could it be your husband's?"

"No, him and I hadn't slept together, in weeks, before Gatlinburg and we haven't since. Look Todd, I'm not trying to obligate you to this baby and I'm sorry you had to find out like this. We can get a DNA test, once she or he is born and go from there."

"How many months are you?"

"Almost five."

"Wow!" he says rubbing his head. "I don't know if I can deal with this right now."

"Do you think this is easy for me? I went to an abortion clinic today. Although I knew I was too far along and never would have gone through with it; I did because the thought of having this baby is scaring the shit out of me. I get that you're upset and confused but don't act like I did this on my own."

"I'm sorry Chloe but I can't do this. We can reschedule the interview; you can use what you already have or trash it all, but I need to get out of here."

I watch him walk out before I get myself together. I go up front and speak to Taylor and the rest of the staff and crew before I leave them and head home.

An hour later, I'm sitting in the middle of my bed, where I've been, since getting home. I've yet to cry because, it wouldn't do any good, anyway. Instead, I continually rub my stomach and sit here.

My phone rings with a call from Kerri.

"Hey K, is everything okay?"

"Cam has been in an accident. She's at Regional One and I don't have all the details, but Ray said they'll meet us there."

"Oh God, Kerri!"

"I know but I'm close to you and can pick you up, in ten minutes."

"I'll be ready."

I get out of bed and change clothes, getting dressed in leggings, t-shirt and tennis shoes. I stop by the bathroom to wash my face. The tears now flow easily as I look in the mirror and began to speak to God out loud.

"God, I know I haven't prayed in a while and I know I'm not living right but right now, I come before you, from the depths of my heart. God, I need you to see about my sister, Cam. God, I don't know what she needs right now, but I'm asking you to guide the hands of the doctors and nurses who are taking care of her.

Please watch over her, my sisters, and our families. Please guide us back to you because we know you are the only one who can forgive and heal us. God, do these things now that I ask of you. Amen."

I hear the doorbell as soon as I'm done. I turn off the lights, in the bedroom before grabbing a jacket and opening the door for Kerri. She walks in and hugs me then she steps back.

"Chloe," she says grabbing my stomach. "Oh my God Chloe, you're pregnant?"

I cry harder.

"Oh sister, why didn't you tell us?"

"I'm scared."

She pulls me into a hug.

"You don't have to be scared, we got you and this baby."

"Okay," I say wiping my face.

"Now, let's go and check on our sister."

I text Ray to let her know we were walking in and she meets us, at the door.

"Hey, have you all heard anything?" we ask while following her to the waiting area.

"No, not yet. We're waiting on Thomas to come out."

"Uh Chloe, what in the heck is this?" Shelby asks, pointing to my stomach, when we walk into the waiting room.

"A baby."

"Bitch," Ray whispers, "you're pregnant and didn't tell us?"

"I know and I'm sorry. I was waiting until the right time. This isn't the right time, but I hadn't expected to see you all tonight and I was tired of trying to hide it."

"Oh, we will be talking about this as soon as we know Camille is good."

"Where's Lyn?" I ask, looking around.

"I don't know, she won't answer her phone."

"That's not like her. Has anyone called Paul?"

"No but I'll call him," Shelby says, walking off.

"There's Thomas," I state, and we all stand.

"Thomas, how is she?"

"I don't know because they're working to stabilize her. The nurse said, they'll come and get me once they're done."

"What happened? Was it a car accident?"

"I'm not sure. I got a call from a nurse telling me to get here."

"Where was she?"

He shrugs. "We had another argument and I asked her to leave. I don't know where she was or what she'd gotten into."

"She tried to call me, but I didn't answer."

"Me either."

Just then Shelby walks up.

"Shelby," Kerri says. "What's wrong? Did you get in touch with Paul?"

"Yea and—Lyn," she pauses.

"Lyn what? Shelby, tell us."

"She was attacked at her store."

Cam

A knock on the door, momentarily pauses me.

"Lady, you alright in there?" she asks.

"Yeah, mind your damn business!"

"Damn lil momma, I was just checking on you," she drags on. "Lady, I don't know what your problem is, but I got something that can make you feel better."

I don't say anything.

"I'm in room eight, if you change your mind."

I go over and snatch the door open.

"Wait, what do you have?"

"How much you got?"

"Money isn't the issue," I snap.

"Fifty dollars," she replies.

"Come in," I tell her, stepping back. "Where is it?"

She pulls a small bag from her shirt.

"No, forget it because it won't help. I'll stick to this vodka. You can go."

"You sure? How do you know if you ain't ever tried it?" she smiles.

"What is it?"

"I call it magic," she laughs, "because it will take your mind off whatever it is that got you like this."

I go over to my purse and pull out the cash. "Here."

I snatch the bag and sit on the bed.

"Put some on your finger and sniff it," she instructs, and I do.

"Now what?"

"You wait," she says shrugging.

"Wait? How long?"

"Lady, give it a minute and you'll feel it."

"I don't have a minute," I tell her, emptying more on my finger and repeating the process with the other nostril.

"Slow down lady."

"Slow down for what?" I laugh, sniffing a little more.

"Stop, you're going to take too much," she says trying to snatch the bag from me.

"You can never have too much magic," I laugh, sniffing more before falling back on the bed. "Whoa, this is some good shit!"

"Hey lady, you ok?" She asks shaking my arm. "Hey! Lady, shit! Hey, wake up!" I hear her scream.

"Damn! Damn!" she keeps saying. "Shit! Man, what the hell should I do? Crap!"

I try to move but I can't.

"Hey, yes I need an ambulance at the Wayside Motel, I think this lady overdosed. I don't know who she is. Yes, she's breathing but barely. Yes, please hurry she's in room 12."

*****

"Ahhh," I scream after a bolt of electricity hits my body." "Stop, that hurts!"

"She's back," a man says. "Make sure her fluids remain steady, keep a watch on her blood pressure, heart rate and temperature to make sure they're coming down.

Give her another dose of benzodiazepine in thirty minutes and if her heart rate or temperature spike again, page me," the male's voice says. "Does she have family here?"

"Yes, her husband is out in the waiting room."

"Send someone out to get him."

"Hello, why can't anyone hear me. Hello, I'm here," I yell.

"Man, why is it always the pretty chicks that end up like this?" I hear a lady asks.

"I don't know," another one replies. "It's sad and I bet she has an entire family who loves her."

"And probably a good ass job."

"SHUT UP! You don't know nothing about me. Just shut up!" I'm screaming before my body starts jerking.

"Wh-at-is-happ-ening, ah—"

"She's having a seizure."

Sometime later, I hear that man's voice again.

"Sir, my name is Dr. Derrick Cleaves."

"Thomas Shannon, how is my wife?"

"Thomas, I'm here," I scream realizing nobody can hear me.

"Would you like to go somewhere else to talk?"

"No, these ladies are her family, so you can talk in front of them."

"The girls are here? Why?" I say, getting angry. "None of them would answer when I needed them."

"Dr. Cleaves, her pressure is spiking again."

"I need to make this quick, but your wife was transported, by ambulance, after being found unconscious. We know, now, that she's suffering from what's called, cocaine toxicity. She was given a dose of Narcan but hasn't regained consciousness."

"Cocaine, are you sure?"

"Yes sir, unfortunately her toxicology report confirmed it."

"What does this mean?"

"She ingested a significant amount of cocaine that caused a spike in her heart rate, body temperature and blood pressure. It also caused the seizure, you witnessed."

"Is she going to die?"

"This can be life threatening but we're doing all we can to stabilize her. Although she is breathing, on her own, we've decided to place her on life support, to take some of the pressure off her heart and other organs. I'm also giving her medicine to try and stabilize everything, but it'll be a while before we know if they were administered in time."

"Is there anything else that can be done?" Thomas asks.

"Unfortunately, all we can do is wait to see what the next twenty-four hours bring. I will not lie, we don't know what kind of internal or brain damage has been done so even if she survives, she may not be the same person you remember."

"Oh my God," Chloe cries.

"For now, we wait and hope her brain wasn't deprived of too much oxygen." Dr. Cleaves replies. "We'll know more once we have the results of all her tests."

"Can we see her?"

"Yes, but not for more than a few minutes because we need to keep her calm. I need you to prepare yourself for what you're going to see, beyond these doors. She has tubes and needles in her body and you all will need to remain calm because even though she hasn't woken up, the stress in the room can still affect her."

"We understand."

"Thank you, Dr. Cleaves."

"I should have all the results, in the morning so we can plan to meet around 10AM in the family room, on this floor, to discuss them." Dr. Cleaves states. "I know this is a lot to take in but she's going to need your strength and prayers."

I feel them surrounding the bed.

"Camille," Thomas chokes up. "Baby, why

couldn't you just get the help you needed? You didn't have to do this. Man! I don't know if you can hear me, but you've got to fight, if not for you, do it for our children."

I feel his tears falling on my hand, but I can't answer. I try to move but I can't.

"Cam, we're here and we need you to fight," Ray says crying.

"Please fight Cam," Kerri says followed by Chloe.

"Yes, we are here for you girl and you've got to come back to us because you're going to be an auntie, again."

"Thomas, I'm here. Sisters, I'm right here. Oh God, what have I done? Please don't let me die like this because I need to make things right." I scream.

"Okay, I'll have to ask you all to leave because her blood pressure is going back up."

"We love you Cam."

When they leave, I feel alone, cold and empty.

Chapter 2

Lyn

I'm sitting in a cold room of Methodist Hospital, watching the doctor and nurses as their lips move. I know they're speaking to me, but I can't hear them.

"Mrs. Williams?"

I look at her.

"My name is Beverly and I'm a forensic nurse, here to ensure you are given the best quality of care while we collect evidence from your body. I know you may be in shock, that's normal after experiencing such a traumatic event. However, my team member will bring you the forms to sign, giving us consent to examine, evaluate the extent of your injuries, collect the evidence and treat you."

I nod.

"Are you ready to begin?"

I nod.

"I need you to say it with your mouth. As I

explained, I will have to ask your permission before moving to the next step and at any time, you want me to stop, say no. Okay?"

"Okay," I reply wiping the tears. "Yes, I'm ready."

With each step and each new yes, I feel more and more violated. I know this has to be done but it's as if, I'm outside of my body. Every time I close my eyes, I try to replay the interactions with Xavier to see if I led him on in anyway but all I see is him on top of me.

"Mrs. Williams, we're done," Beverly says. "Here's some clothes for you to get dressed in. In a moment, I'll bring you some medications for emergency contraception and to try and prevent any sexually transmitted diseases. The doctor will also come in to suture that gash on your neck."

I only nod.

She turns to walk out but comes back.

"Can I pray for you?"

I look at her.

"I know it isn't customary, but you've suffered a serious trauma and I feel the need to pray for you.

Will that be okay?"

"Yes."

She grabs my hands but before she speaks, the other nurses in the room begin to remove their gloves. They surround the bed and lock hands.

"Dear God, as I stand here, holding the hand of my sister, I ask for your power to speak. God, she needs you and because you've connected us, use me. Use me, like never before, to speak peace and understanding during this difficult situation.

God, she's been violated and left as a victim, but I need you to wash away her shame. Father, her body has been bruised but I need you to make it better. Father, her strength and virtue have taken a beating, but I need you to restore.

Stop the thoughts of guilt and remove the what-ifs because this was evil's doing and not hers. This is why I had to come and speak over her life. Mrs. Williams, this was not your fault, it was evilness trying to win. Mrs. Williams, nothing you could have done would have prevented this, it was the evilness of a man.

Yet, I'm praying for you, my sister that in the minutes and days to come, you will not lose faith and hope. For we serve a God who has the power to restore what man tried to break. Do it for her God, not tomorrow but right now.

Give her understanding, rock her in the midnight hour and comfort her so that when she closes her eyes, she'll know; evil didn't win. I thank you Father and this I pray. Amen."

She pulls me into a hug and I sob, on her shoulders.

Shelby

I rush into the hospital, but I'm stopped by security.

"Ma'am, you need to sign in. What is the patient's name?"

"Lynesha Williams. L-Y-N-E-S-H-A," I tell her, trying to calm down.

"I need your driver's license."

I hand it to her and a few minutes later, she is handing me a sticker. She tells me to follow the signs to the Emergency Department. When I get to the nurses' station, she points me to the room.

I knock and hear Paul's voice, saying to come in. I push open the door to see Lyn sitting on the side of the bed, in scrubs. I go over to her and throw my arms around her. She jumps.

"I'm here sister."

She doesn't respond, instead she just stares ahead.

A nurse knocks on the door and ask us to step out, momentarily. I touch her hand before walking out.

When the door close, I turn to Paul.

"How long has she been like that?"

"Since I got here."

"What happened?"

He looks at me, with tears in his eyes.

"I should have been there, but I was too late and," he pauses, "he'd already attacked her."

He punches the wall.

"Paul, stop. Lyn is going to need you but not like this."

"Shelby, I messed everything up," he cries. "I messed everything up."

I hold his arm and wait until he calms down.

"What do you mean? This wasn't your fault."

"It is because she never would have been there, had it not been for—" he pauses.

"For what?"

"I should have been there," he resigns, shaking his head.

"Do they know who did this?"

"Yes, and he's at the morgue because Lyn killed him."

"Lord Jesus," I say leaning against the wall. "Can this night get any worse?"

"Excuse me, my name is Detective Frank Radar and I'm looking for Lynesha Williams."

"I'm her husband and she's in with the nurse right now. What can I do for you?"

"Sir, I know your wife has been through a traumatic ordeal, tonight but I need to ask her a few questions."

"Can't this wait until tomorrow?" I question.

"Unfortunately, it can't."

"Well, you can question her once she has a lawyer present." Paul tells him.

"That's fine," Detective Radar states. "You can have him or her meet us downtown, but I'll have to transport Mrs. Williams." He moves over to the nurses' station.

"Do you have a lawyer?" I ask.

"No," he shakes his head. "I've been trying to call Cam."

"Paul, Cam is in ICU at Regional One. She overdosed, tonight."

"Cam did what?" Lyn asks, standing at the door we hadn't realized was open. "Shelby, what happened to Cam?"

"She was found unconscious in a hotel room after overdosing. That's all I've been told."

"Let's go," she says.

"We can't," Paul says moving over to Lyn.

"Don't touch me," she snaps at him.

"Lyn, I know you're upset but there is a detective here to take you downtown for questioning."

"They'll have to wait because I'm going to check on my friend."

"I'm sorry ma'am but it isn't that simple," the detective says. "You will need to come with us."

"This is some bullshit!" Lyn screams. "That man attacked me but you're treating me like the criminal."

"Lyn baby just calm down and go with them. I'll be right behind you."

"No, fuck you Paul. I don't want you anywhere near me. Go home to your other family and leave me alone."

She has tears streaming down her face as I look from her to Paul.

"Shelby," she says getting my attention. "Can you come with me?"

"Sure, I'll meet you down there. Detective Radar, where are you taking her?"

"To Felony Response on Adams. Here's the address. You can meet us there."

"Lyn," Paul calls out, but she keeps walking.

When I get to the car, I call Thomas and put it on speaker.

"Thomas, hey, how is Cam?"

"They are working to stabilize her but she's on life support."

I gasp.

"She's breathing on her own but she's suffering from cocaine toxicity and the next 24 hours will be crucial. We're meeting with the doctor at ten, tomorrow morning."

"I'll be there but, in the meantime, is there anything I can do?"

"No. My parents are with the children and I'm going to stay here. How is Lyn?"

"That's what I'm calling about. She was attacked at her store and she killed the guy who did it. They are taking her to Felony Response, on Adams St. and she needs an attorney."

"I'll call someone who will meet her there. His name is Lionel Peoples."

"Thanks Thomas and call me, if anything changes."

"You too."

I lay my head back on the seat, exhausted before I put the address into the GPS and drive off.

Chloe

"Has anybody talked to Shelby?" I ask, as we're walking to the car.

"She just responded to my text. She says they are headed to the police station because Lyn has to answer some questions," Ray says before gasping. "Oh my God, she killed him."

"She killed who?" Kerri and I ask, at the same time.

"Lyn killed the guy who attacked her."

Kerri burst into tears. "What is happening to us? It seems like everything is falling apart, for all of us, at one time. Do you think it's God punishing us?"

"I'm not into church, as well as I should be, but I know God doesn't work like this," I tell them. "What this is, it's part life and part evil. Yes, I think we could all get more familiar with God, but we can't blame Him for this. Everything we're going through, except

Lyn, is due to our own foolishness."

"Then we've got to do better. We've got to evaluate our lives and do better because I don't know if I can take anything else," Kerri adds.

"Shelby is going to take Lyn home, once their done but she says there's something going on with her and Paul. She isn't sure if Lyn will go home or with her, but she'll let us know." Ray tells us, after reading her texts.

I sigh. "I never thought, in a million years, we'd be here. Cam is on life support and fighting for her life, Lyn being attacked and our marriages over or in trouble. Life has a way of getting your attention, doesn't it?"

"God does," Ray corrects. "We get so comfortable with the way things are that when trouble does happen, it catches us off guard. And just maybe, God is allowing each of us to face trouble, together as a way to heal together."

"I just wish it could have been a different way, though because this, what we're facing now, it's a lot."

"Yea, but would we have listened had it not been? Look at us," I say, "we're all ready, right now, to pray heaven down but a few hours ago, we barely said our grace. So, the answer isn't what's happening to us but what happened to us. There was a time when God was first in our lives and home."

"You're right Chloe but truthfully, I don't know where to begin."

"There was something I read on Facebook, a few days ago," Ray says opening her phone. "It says, God isn't moved by our desperation, but He will be moved by our devotion. I don't know about y'all but I'm in a place where I need God, more than ever."

"We all do because you heard the doctor. It's out of his hands."

"What would make Cam do cocaine, though? Do y'all think that's what she was on, in LA?" Kerri asks.

"Had you asked me, a few weeks ago, I probably would have said no, but Cam has been wilding lately. Who knows what all she's gotten into? However, I don't believe she intentionally overdosed because she loves life, too much."

"This just doesn't make sense."

"No, it doesn't but maybe it isn't for us to understand." Ray says, sighing. "Y'all go home, try to get some rest and I'll see you all in the morning."

*****

"Kerri, thanks for dropping me off," I say, grabbing my keys from my purse when she pulls up in front of the house.

"You're welcome. Try to rest and don't think I've forgotten about the surprise, you sprung on us. I can't believe you've been hiding your pregnancy, this entire time. If you weren't pregnant, I'd kick your butt," she laughs.

"I haven't, trust me. Text and let me know you made it home." I say closing the car door.

I make it into the house, turn the alarm on and head to the bedroom. My phone vibrates in my hand.

Thinking, it's probably one of the girls, I quickly check it but it's a text from Todd.

TODD: Chloe, I know it's late, but can we talk?

"Really," I say out loud, deciding to wait before I reply back. I undress and shower before getting into the bed. Once I'm comfortable, I grab the phone.

ME: Yes, but not tonight.

TODD: Chloe, I'm sorry for walking out on you because you didn't deserve that. If you give me the chance, I'd like to apologize in person. I'll be in Memphis until tomorrow.

ME: Thank you and you're right but you had every right to be upset. I apologize for keeping this from you.

TODD: Will you please call me tomorrow, so we can talk.

ME: Tomorrow isn't good, for me but I'll try.

TODD: Thanks, and goodnight Chloe.

I put the phone on the nightstand and slide down under the comforter. When my body finally settles, I release the tears.

"God, I don't know what's happening and I don't understand but I trust your plan. Please take care of Lyn and Cam and this little one, you're trusting me with. Amen."

Kerri

The house is dark and quiet by the time I make it home. I send Chloe a text before checking the couch to see if Michael is there, but he isn't. I go to MJ's room and kneel beside his bed, kissing him on the forehead.

"You okay?" Michael asks, causing me to jump.

"Yea," I whisper, wiping the tears and getting up. "Where were you?"

"In the bathroom but what's going on? Why are you crying?"

"Michael, I've had a long night. I know I said we can finish the conversation, but I don't have the energy."

"Kerri, please tell me what happened?"

"Cam overdosed and is in ICU, not sure if she's going to survive and Lyn was attacked, at her store." I tell him when he follows me into the bedroom. "I just don't understand how we got here."

He walks over and wraps his arms around me as I burst into tears.

"A year ago, we were all happy and enjoying life. Not just you and me but all of us. Now, there's talk of divorce, chaos, overdose—what happened to us?"

"Kerri, I wish I had the right words to remove this weight, but I don't because, truthfully, my selfishness has played a part in it. These last few months, I became someone I didn't recognize and that wasn't fair to you or MJ. However, I meant what I said before. I'm working to change that and I'm going to show you."

I sit on the bed. "I appreciate you saying that but there are some underlying issues, you need to address and maybe you need to start with rehab or at least a therapist."

"You're right and after you left tonight, I did some research and made some calls. The first was to our people help hotline, through the job. They made me see, I have a problem.

Then I talked to my boss who is allowing me a thirty day, leave of absence. I also made some calls to some rehab facilities, the helpline referred me too. There's one in Jackson, MS, an inpatient facility, and they have space for me. I leave, Thursday morning."

"Wow, I don't know what to say."

"Kerri, there is a lot of emotional baggage, from my past, that I need to deal with. I've always known it was there but seeing you, building this business triggered some abandonment issues. I know I said it was because of my dad and although it played a part, I've never really dealt with my mom leaving.

It took seeing you with another man, to realize how bad I'd screwed up and just how much I love you. I'm so sorry Kerri. Will you forgive me?"

"Michael, I love you too but forgiving you is going to take some time. I wish I could forget about everything, at this very moment but truth is, you hurt. I've been there, with you, for everything and all I needed was you, but you left. I want to be able to trust you, knowing you won't run every time something happens and right now, I can't."

"I understand but will you at least think about it because I can't do this without you."

"Yes, you can. Michael, I don't want you to do this for me. You need to get healthy and whole, for you because what's to say, you and I don't work out. Will you go back to drinking? Look, go to rehab and deal with your emotional issues, in order for you to heal. Then maybe you'll be able to love me and MJ, the way we deserve. Can you promise me that?"

"I do."

"Good," I say hugging him. "I don't know what God has planned for us, Michael but if you put forth an effort, I'd like to see where our marriage stands. This doesn't mean, we will pick up where we left off, but we'll see, once you're fully sober."

"Thank you, Kerri."

"Where are you staying?"

"At an extended stay, down the street."

"Well, the guestroom is yours, until you leave

because I am sure MJ would love to see you when he wakes up in the morning."

He stands and walks toward the door but turns back. "What about your boyfriend?"

"First off, he isn't my boyfriend. He was a distraction, one I wouldn't have needed had you— you know what, you're not to blame for my stupidity because I didn't have to sleep with him. I made that mistake and I own it but what happened between Adrian and I, was one time and it's over."

He smiles.

"I didn't end things because of you, I ended it for me. Good night Michael."

"Goodnight Kerri and I'm praying for Cam and Lyn. Oh, do you think I can get a key to the house?"

"Look in the drawer in the kitchen."

Ray

I walk into the house and it's, surprisingly, quiet. I reset the alarm and drop my purse on the kitchen counter, before getting my phone and going into the bedroom.

I shower, turn the light off and get into bed.

"Mom, are you asleep?" Rashida asks, sometime later, standing next to the bed causing me to jump.

"No, what's wrong?"

"Can I talk to you?"

"Sure," I respond, turning on the bedside light and sitting up.

"Is dad gay?" she asks with tears in her eyes. "Is that why y'all are getting a divorce?"

"Uh," I say, my mouth suddenly dry. "What, um, why would you ask that?"

"I was using dad's computer, a few weeks ago and I saw some—"

"Some what?" Justin questions, from the door

causing both of us to jump. "And why were you on my computer?"

"You told me I could use it, to get some pictures for the yearbook. I wasn't going through your stuff, but I saw some pictures and—are you gay?"

We both wait for him to answer.

"Rashida, yes. Yes, I'm gay."

She burst into tears and runs out the room.

I get out of bed to go after her but first, I turn back to him.

"What kinds of pictures do you have on your computer that would make our daughter believe you're gay?"

"I didn't know they were on there because I thought I'd deleted all of them."

"Damn it, Justin. What kind of pictures?"

"Of me and Travis. He took them, one night when—"

"Please spare me the details."

"I'm sorry. I realized I've made a mess of this

family but I'm tired of apologizing. Yes, I'm gay and I can't help it."

"Who asked you to help it? Huh? All I've ever asked was for you to be honest with me and for the last sixteen years, you've been anything but that."

"I have been honest with you because I've never acted on my desires, not until Travis."

"Oh, that makes it better," I say with sarcasm. "Justin, how long have you been gay?"

"What difference does that make?"

"It makes all the difference. Answer the question. No, better yet, why did you marry me?"

"Ray, this has nothing to do with you."

"This has every freaking thing to do with me so don't play me like I'm stupid. Why did you marry me?"

"Because you were pregnant," he yells before sighing, loudly.

"Wow, this keeps getting better."

"When I met you, I was in a rough place, in my life. I was dealing with my mom who was pressuring me to settle down. She said, me being gay was a phase."

"Wait, your mom knew you were gay?"

"Yes, she'd known since I was fourteen."

"No wonder I've never liked her, Oprah Winfrey looking ass," I say. "All these years, you've both been lying to me."

"That's not fair because it wasn't her place to tell you, it was mine."

"You're right but she knew I was marrying her lying ass son and she also knew you were marrying me for all the wrong reasons."

"I wanted to do right by you and our child but then you lost the baby."

"Why didn't you divorce me, then?"

"I saw how heavy the toil of losing our first child was on you and I couldn't leave you like that. Six months later, you were pregnant with Rashida."

I wipe the tears. "Did you ever love me or was I just a stand in while you built this perfect life, for yourself?"

"To be honest, I grew to love you. I apologize if that came out harsh but it's my truth. You have to know, Raylan, I never expected to even sleep with you. The night, I met you in that café, on campus, my mom and I had gotten into a heated argument over my lifestyle. She'd caught me with this boy, I liked, and she called me all kinds of names.

She told me, as long as I was gay, I'd never be anything and the only way, she'd ever accept me; I couldn't be that way. That night, I was going to commit suicide, but I stopped by that café and you were there. You must have sensed something was wrong because you struck up a conversation with me."

"You still had ample time to tell me because we didn't sleep together, that night."

"I know but we started hanging out. We'd talk for hours and it was as if, you were sent to save me. You have to understand Ray. My mother always said this was a phase and meeting you, I thought she was right. Anyway, you remember the frat party we went too?"

"The night you found out; you didn't cross. What does that have to do with anything?"

"Truthfully, I did cross, but I declined to join because the leader of the fraternity was the guy I was secretly dating. I knew there was no way I could stay in the same house with him. I got drunk that night and when you invited me back to your room, we slept together."

"And I got pregnant."

"When my mom found out, she said we had to get married."

"I've heard enough," I tell him. "You can go."

"Ray, please."

"Please what? Please what, Justin?"

"Please forgive me."

I laugh. "Forgive you? Forgive you for lying? Or maybe I should forgive you for using me as a stand-in, all these years? Or the worse of them all, forgive you for breaking mine and our children's hearts? Well, hell no. I don't forgive you and I pray, you'll one day feel the same amount of pain, you've caused us."

I walk out and leave him standing there.

Cam

I open my eyes and look around, but I don't see anyone or hear anything.

"Hello," I call out but all I get is silence. I slowly move to see if I can and when I do, I throw the covers back and swing my feet, over the side of the bed until they hit the cold floor.

"Hello," I call out again. "Is anyone here? Where am I?"

It's dark so I feel my way until my hand hits something. I feel around and touch a door knob. I turn it and it opens into the inside a house.

I step out.

"Wait," I say out loud, "this is my house."

I walk a little farther, confused until I hear music.

"Thomas, TJ, Courtney; where is everybody?"

Just then Thomas comes through the door. "Oh, thank God," I say letting out the nervous breath, I'd been holding but he walks right pass me. "Thomas, come on. I know you're still mad at me but say something."

"Hey babe, were you able to find some cranberry sauce?"

I turn at the sound of a woman's voice. When he moves away from her, I realize its Chelle's voice.

"Yeah, at Walgreens. I got two, just in case."

"Thanks. Will you go and let everybody know it's time to eat?" she asks before kissing him and this time, when she turns, I see her pregnant stomach.

A few minutes later, my daughter Courtney comes down the hall, followed by my son, TJ.

"What the—hello, what are y'all doing?" I scream.

"Mom, this food smells great," TJ tells her. "What do you need help with?"

"You can get that pitcher of tea and those glasses."

I watch, with tears in my eyes, as they along with Shelby, Lyn, Ray, Kerri, Chloe and their families; sit around the table. Thomas says grace and they all begin to eat.

"Happy Thanksgiving everyone," Chelle says. "Sticking with the tradition, we started last year, I'll go first with what I'm thankful for. I'm thankful for life and love. I had no idea, when I met Thomas that a year later, we'd be married and having a baby," she pauses. "I guess I should thank Cam because if it wasn't for her, I never would have met my good thang. Thank you, Cam," she says raising her glass.

"I guess I should thank Cam too," Thomas laughs. "She taught me what I didn't want in a wife. God rests her soul."

TJ clears his throat. "Well, I want to thank Chelle for being a great mom to us. When Cam died, from that drug overdose, I was hurt at how selfish she was. She didn't care about anyone but herself and she left us to fend for ourselves.

Then you came along, and I saw how happy you made our dad and you were willing to step in and raise us and for that I'm grateful. We couldn't have asked for a better replacement."

Courtney rolls her eyes. "Do I have to sit here and listen to this crap?"

"Courtney, watch your mouth," Thomas berates her. "This is Thanksgiving and you will not ruin it."

"Thanksgiving," she laughs. "Who has something to be thankful for? Other than TJ's lame ass. Huh? Look around because I don't see anything but misery and this fake love crap. Mom is dead and you're sitting here acting as if she never existed. You know what? I'm done with this."

"No, you're not because you're under my care and if you think—"

"What are you going to do? Call the police again?" she laughs. "Well screw you and this dinner." She throws a finger sign before storming out.

I follow her. "Courtney, wait. Please baby, I'm right here."

She walks down the street to another house. Going around the back, she lets herself inside this rundown shed.

"Hey," the boy says. "I thought you'd be at home eating turkey."

"Man forget that. How am I supposed to sit around a table and be happy about the way my life is?"

"Girl, stop complaining because your dad could have left your ass in that rehab, over the holiday."

"I wish he would have because then I wouldn't be out here, sober. At least in rehab, they keep you medicated to forget your problems."

"Well, I can help with that, if you want me too," he tells her.

"Hell yea, what you got?"

"What are you in the mood for?"

"Something that will take me away from here," she tells him.

"Then I have just the thing." I watch as he goes over to a picture, hanging on the wall. He removes a piece from the front of it, to show a secret compartment. From there he pulls out a bag.

"What is it?" Courtney asks, and he smiles.

"Exactly what you asked for. I call it magic."

"NO," I scream. "Courtney, no!"

My body begins to shake, and I can't control it, but I feel it.

"She's having a seizure," I hear a woman say before everything goes dark.

Chapter 3

Lyn

"Lynesha—"

"Please call me Lyn."

"Lyn, my name is Lionel Peoples and Thomas asked me to take care of you. Before the detectives come in, I want to make sure you're okay."

"No, I'm not okay. I was attacked and raped by some filthy, disgusting human being while my friend is fighting for her life in ICU and I'm stuck here. It's not fair. I shouldn't be here, being treated like a criminal."

"Lyn, I understand your frustration but the sooner we can get this over with, the better. I need you to understand something, I'm on your side and I need you to trust me. If I say, stop talking, stop. If I tell you not to answer, don't."

I nod.

The door opens, and two people come in.

"Mrs. Williams, I'm Sgt. Jovita Berks and you've

met Detective Frank Radar. We're with the Memphis Police Department Homicide Division. You are not under arrest however; I must read your Miranda rights.

You have the right to remain silent, anything you say can and will be used against you, in a court of law. You have the right to an attorney. If you cannot afford an attorney, one will be provided to you. Do you understand these rights as I have read them to you?"

"Yes."

"I need you to sign and date, here."

"Now, Mrs. Williams, please tell us what happened this afternoon." Sgt. Berks says.

I wipe the falling tears.

"I'd been at my boutique during inventory because the store is closed today, and I can usually get a lot done. Around four, I had someone to stop by, unexpectedly."

"Who?" the detective asks.

"A lady who says she was having an affair with my husband. Kandis, something. Anyway, my husband showed up and I asked them both to leave. My husband was constantly calling and when I heard the bell ring, at the back door, I thought it was them again. It wasn't."

"What time did the assailant show up?" Detective Radar inquires.

"It wasn't long afterwards, which is why I opened the door without checking who it was."

"Did you know him, or had you seen him before today?" Sgt. Berks asks.

"Yea. His name is Xavier and he'd been delivering to the store for about, two months. A few weeks back, he came to the store, late saying he'd forgotten a box. He made a pass at me, but I turned him down. Days later, he came back."

"What happened?"

"Same thing, he'd forgotten to deliver one of my boxes. He came on to me again, but my husband showed up."

"Did you tell your husband about him?'

"No because for a minute, I liked the attention but then I came to my senses. I asked him to stop and I called and left a message for his manager, but he never called back."

"What happened tonight?"

"Like I said, my husband's mistress stopped by and after I put them out, I was pissed. So, when he showed up, I let him in. He kissed me, or I kissed him, and I didn't stop him, at first but when I did, he turned angry.

He called me a tease and said something about me trying to get him fired. I apologized, and he turned, like he was leaving but he pulled a knife instead. I tried to run but he grabbed me by my hair, twisting it in his hand."

My leg is shaking so fast that I can't seem to control it. I start to rock back and forth. "I begged him to stop pulling my hair because it was hurting so bad. He said he would, if I stopped fighting."

I did.

He then threw me on the ground, cut off my panties and had his hand under my neck. He said if I moved again, he'd slit my throat and to know he wasn't playing, he cut me." I stop talking when I realize I have my hand on my neck.

"He then, um, he removed himself, entered me and every time he grunted, he would squeeze harder. I couldn't breathe. I could smell the blood, falling to the floor beneath me."

"Do you need a break?"

I shake my head no, wiping the tears. "He must have laid the knife on my back because I heard it drop. When it did, I relaxed, like I was enjoying it. He started talking and," I take a deep breath, "slapping me on the butt. He was grunting, and I knew he—um, he was close to climaxing. When he closed his eyes, I grabbed the knife and stabbed him in the neck. He fell, I hit the panic button and a few minutes later, my husband Paul was opening the door."

"Where you and the assailant having an affair?"

"No, I told you he'd come on to me but that's it," I say getting angry. "I didn't ask for this."

"Are there any more questions, Sgt.? My client has gone through something I wouldn't wish on my worst enemy and she needs to be with her family."

"One more. Mrs. Williams, are there any security cameras, in your business that can corroborate the details of your attack?"

"Yes, but I'm not lying."

"I know and I'm not insinuating you are."

"I can give you my login information and you can pull the videos."

She passes me a pen and pad.

"Are we done?" I ask.

"We are, and I am sorry for what happened to you. Here is a card for the rape crisis center. They have counselors, on staff, who can help you deal with the aftermath of this kind of trauma."

"Aftermath?" I repeat. "Like what happens after a storm?"

"Yes, but just like any storm, after the damage then comes restoration." Sgt. Berks tells me.

I look at her and my tears become sobs. The attorney moves, and she comes around the table.

"Lyn, I know you've been through hell, but you can survive this. Please believe me because I've been there. It's going to be hard, at first and for a while but if you're willing to heal; you will."

"Thank you."

"Thank you, Sgt. Becker. Please call my office if you need to speak to my client further. Let's go Lyn."

I get home and the house is quiet. I drop my things, next to the door, turn on the alarm and go into my bedroom.

I strip out of the scrubs, I was given at the hospital, and get into the shower. As the visions of this day, replays like it's on four times the speed, in rewind, I slink into the corner of the tub and scream.

Shelby

I drag into the house, after dropping Lyn off at home. I tried to convince her, to let me stay but she wanted to be alone.

I called Jo to let her know some of what's going on and that the boutique would be closed, for a while.

I stop by the nursery to check on Brinae, and she's still asleep. I stand there, for a minute, as tears flow.

"God, how did we get here?"

"Babe," Brian says from the door. "Are you okay?"

"I will be."

I rub the baby's forehead and walk out, pass him.

"You want something to eat? I can fix us some eggs and toast seeing that the sun is coming up."

"No, I don't have an appetite."

I start to undress before going to take a shower. Once I'm done, I turn out the light in the bathroom and walk out.

"Shelby, can we please talk?"

I climb into the bed, while he sits at the end.

"I talked to Thomas and he told me what's going on with Camille and Lyn. All while you were gone, I've been replaying the last few weeks and I want you to know, I'm sorry.

Just thinking about Thomas and what he must be going through, as he watches his wife lying there not knowing if she will wake up; makes me sick at the stomach."

"Brian don't go there because Cam will make it through this," I say as tears run down my face.

"I know she will Shelby, but what I'm saying is, tonight made me think of how foolish I've been. When I heard the pain in Thomas' voice because he didn't understand what happened, to his wife who was healthy one moment and hooked up to machines, the next; it was an eye opener. Had something happened to me before I had a chance to tell you everything, man," he sighs. "I'm sorry."

"Why did it take that, though? We've been through mistakes, infidelity, loss, happiness and whatever else; because we were young and neither of us were perfect. Yet, we made it. We haven't faked it, we made it because we worked hard to be what each other needed.

Then, in your darkest moment, you didn't even come to me. You pushed me away. Why? Why was it easier, for you to run when we've always counted on each other?" I ask him.

"Honestly, it had nothing to do with you."

I throw my hands up. "Famous bullshit line. Oh, I'm sick and possibly dying but it has nothing to do with you, Shelby." I mimic with a deep voice.

"Shelby, you have to understand how hard this is, for me."

"How am I supposed to understand when I don't know what this is? You've been going to doctor's appointments and everything, without saying one word to me. Tell me how I'm supposed to understand."

"I was selfish, and I'll apologize every day and twice on Sunday but right now, I need you because," he chokes up, "I'm scared Shelby. I am terrified of leaving you and our daughter."

He begins to sob and at first, the anger won't allow me to move but I do. I take his hand and pull him to me.

"I'm so sorry," he cries. "I'm so sorry."

He lays his head on my lap and we stay that way for a few minutes before he sits up.

"I should have been honest with you, from the moment I found out, but truth is, I couldn't say it out loud."

"Well, I need you to find your voice, now."

"The doctor thinks I have Glioblastoma, which is an aggressive cancer found in the brain or spinal cord."

"Thinks?"

"I have to see an oncologist, in two weeks, who will give me the results of my MRI. Right now, all I know is, there's a tumor pressing on my brain. He said, it could have been there since birth but it's getting bigger which is causing my headaches."

"So, what do you do in the mean time?"

"I have medicine that helps with the pain and nausea and as long as it's controlled, I wait until my next appointment. But Shelby, I can't do this without you."

He squeezes my hand.

"I'll be there but I'm really disappointed in the way you handled this."

"I know."

"And we've got to get back in church," I tell him. "I know this is usually the time when people flock to God, but we used to be faithful."

"I agree. I saw a sign, yesterday for the church, not far from here. I think it's called High Point. Maybe we can check it out."

"We should."

He pulls me towards him, hugging me until I can

feel his heart beating through his shirt. I wrap my arms around him and he begins to cry.

"Brian, can I pray for us?"

He nods yes, so I close my eyes.

"Dear God, please forgive us. Forgive us for trying to do this journey of life, alone. God, we need you as the head of our family because we've messed things up. Father, I hope you can hear me and forgive us because we need you to heal. Heal my husband, Camille and Lyn, making them better from the inside out.

Then God, give strength, right now. Not just to us but to every one of my sisters because you are the only one who can get us through this. There are tough times ahead but with you, we can make it. Please God. Amen."

He looks at me and smile. "It's been a long time since we prayed together."

"I know and that, along with some other stuff changes, tonight. No more secrets," I tell him.

"No more secrets."

Meeting with the doctor (Shelby)

"Good Morning," the doctor says coming in and my mouth drops. "My name is Dr. Derrick Cleaves and this is Chaplain Magnolia Reeves."

He looks at me and I quickly turn my head.

"Chaplain? Why is there a chaplain?" Ray questions. "Did something happen?"

"Ma'am, I apologize if my presence insinuates something horrible, it doesn't. We know how hard it can be, when a family is sitting where you are, so we want to offer you any resource that can help you cope."

"And to add to what Chaplain Reeves has stated, it's customary, for me, to have a chaplain present, whenever I talk to family members because I believe in the power or prayer."

We all let out a sigh of relief, as Dr. Cleaves continues. "Now, I know you're Thomas but who else do we have here?"

"These are some of Camille's best friends," Thomas says, introducing each of us. "You can speak freely."

"Mr. Shannon, your wife made it through the night, which is a good sign and it lets us know, she's fighting. However, I won't give you false hope because she isn't out of the woods. She suffered another seizure on last night, so we had to up her medication.

Her latest CAT Scan does not show any signs of brain damage, but we'll still need to assess her mental capacity and organ function, once she wakes up." Dr. Cleaves explains.

"Why the ventilator?" Thomas questions.

"To take some pressure off of her organs. With cocaine toxicity, her body's functions are increased as though she's been given a heavy dose of adrenaline. We have to counter that with medication and hope we did so in time."

"What are the next steps?"

"We wait. She will remain in ICU until she regains consciousness so that she can be monitored closely and if she wakes—"

"When," Chloe interjects.

"I'm sorry."

"You said if, like it's a possibility. No sir, when Cam wakes up, because she will."

"When she wakes up, we'll know more," he finishes.

"Dr. Cleaves, I hear what Chloe said but, in all honesty, do you think she will wake up?" Kerri asks.

"I do, but I need to be absolutely sure you all understand. We don't know how long she was unconscious before she was brought in, so I don't know if she will have any lasting effects from this," he replies. "All we can do is wait and pray."

"Can we see her?" I ask.

"Yes, but don't overwhelm her with a lot of noise in the room. You can talk to her, but not too much. We want to keep her blood pressure and heart rate down."

"Thank you Dr. Cleaves. I really appreciate all you've done for my wife," Thomas said, standing to shake his hand.

"You are welcome, and it is good to see a family that wants the best for their loved one. If you have any questions, please don't hesitate to call. We will speak again in the coming days," he says.

"May we pray before you leave?" Chaplain Reeves asks. We all stand and join hands.

"Our Heavenly Father, we come to you, from the gratefulness of our hearts. God, we thank you for this family and even though, sickness got us here, we still trust you. God, you heard the report of the doctor, but we stand on your word that says, we can ask of you and you'll do it. Well God, we need you to heal their sister, today. You know the condition she's in, but we still know your power.

In your time, God, heal and bring her back, better than she was before. Then, don't just stop there, guide this family. Allow them to bind together and not apart. Give them strength to endure the rough days ahead and when it's all done, give them a testimony that they'll never be ashamed to tell. We thank you Father and amen."

"Amen."

"Dr. Cleaves, can I talk to you for a moment?" I ask as we all get ready to leave.

"Sure, I have a few moments," he replies.

"You all can go ahead, and I'll meet you in Cam's room."

As soon as the door closes, I cross my arms.

"How long have you been back in the city?"

"I've been back about six months and you would have known had you answered my calls."

"I didn't have a reason to answer you."

"Shelby, I get that we left things, in a bad spot but we can discuss that later. Are you okay?" he questions, walking closer to me.

"Yes, and although I'm not happy to see you, I do feel better knowing you're the one taking care of my sister. I can't imagine losing her," I tell him.

He smiles before pulling me in for a kiss.

"Stop, we can't do that."

"I know but I've missed you."

"Whatever. Just make sure you take care of Camille."

"I'm doing all I can to make sure she is okay. Do you all have any idea what happened? The police said she was found in a motel, off Summer. She doesn't look like the type to hang in that part of town."

"We really don't know but Cam has been acting differently, these last few months. Wild, I should say."

"You don't think this was intentional, do you?"

"God no. Knowing Cam, the way I do, this was her acting out and she got carried away."

"I just hope this doesn't cost her any lasting effects."

"Me either."

"Shelby, I'm glad I get to see you, I just wish it wasn't under these circumstances. Can we do lunch or something, soon?"

"Derrick, that's not a good idea because I have a lot going on, right now. However, the mistake we made, years ago, cannot happen again."

"I understand, and I'll respect that but know I'm here for you."

"Thank you but let me get back before they start asking questions."

"You never told them about us?"

"No and I have no plans to do so now but thank you again. I really appreciate all that you're doing." I say as he kisses me on the cheek.

As we're coming out the room, Ray is walking down the hall, on the phone.

"Thank you again Dr. Cleaves," I say reaching to shake his hand.

"You're welcome. If you have any questions, please call."

"You ole sneaky heifer, how long have you been messing with that man?" Ray asks, intertwining her arm into mine.

"I don't know what you're talking about, Raylan.

That man is Cam's doctor."

"Don't Raylan me because I saw the way you two were looking at each other. I'm shocked no one else did."

"Fine," I sigh. "He and I slept together, a few years ago. It was during a time Brian and I weren't in a good space. However, before you say anything, Brian knows about the affair. I told him after Derrick moved away."

"Are you going to tell him that he's back?"

"Hell no. I'm going to let that sleeping dog lay. Besides, I don't have any plans on seeing him, anymore. Now, if you're done."

"Oh, I'm done if you are," she smiles.

Lyn

"Good morning, how can I help you?"

"Good morning, I am trying to find a room number for a patient."

"Name?"

"Camille Shannon," I reply.

"She's in the ICU, room 2002 but you have about forty-five minutes before the next visiting hour. Take the second set of elevators to the third floor. When you get off, there should be someone there to sign you in and you will need some form of identification."

I sign in and find a seat in the waiting area until visiting hours. I have my head in my hands, when I hear someone calling my name.

"Lyn, are you okay?"

"Thomas, hey, what did you say?" I ask him.

"I asked, if you were okay?"

I smile before standing up to give him a hug. "Yea, I'm good but how are you and the kids?"

"We're holding on to hope."

"Cam is strong, and she'll survive this," I reassure him.

"I just hope, she survives with her mind intact."

We both sit.

"Why would Cam do this?" he asks, not to me in particular but I understood. "I never saw the signs of this. I mean, she used enough cocaine to stop her heart and all I want to know is why."

"Thomas, I wish I could answer that, but no one is to blame, for Cam's actions but her. We've tried to talk some sense into her, but she would not listen."

"Don't I know. The only reason she was at that motel, is because I put her out. Well, I gave her a choice of help or the door."

"She chose the latter," I finish his sentence. "Addicts do that, but I know that we are not to blame."

His phone rings.

"I need to take this, but it was good seeing you."

When he leaves, I sit back in the chair and close my eyes.

"We've been in a relationship for over three years. It started off as sex and an occasional dinner but after first six months, things evolved.

He also comes home to me; we take family vacation and pictures too. Lyn, I know this is a lot to take in, but Paul said, he's only staying because you're unstable.

You're a tease and you can't keep playing with people's emotions and bitch, today you're going to be more than sorry. Turn around, lift that dress and remove your panties."

I jump when someone touches me, pulling me from the thoughts of yesterday that are all running together.

"Ma'am, are you okay?"

I jump up, without answering as I try to find the nearest restroom. Barreling into the first stall, I lean against the wall, covering my mouth as the tears flood in.

"God, I can't do this on my own," I whisper.

"Please help me."

I stay in that stall, for a while before coming out. I wash my hands and head back to the waiting room.

"Miss, visiting hours have started," the lady at the desk tells me. "Go through those doors."

"Thank you."

I walk into the room, to see Cam lying there with all of those machines and tubes and it feels like the breath is being pulled from my lungs. Taking her hand, "Cam, it's Lyn. I'm here," I tell her as tears flow.

"Girl, never in a hundred, sleepless nights would I have imagined you here, not like this. Sister, you've got to wake up. You hear me? You don't get to leave us like this."

I sit down, in the chair next to her bed and lay my head on her hand.

"Excuse me, I don't mean to interrupt but I need to get some blood from her," the nurse says.

"Sure, do you need me to leave?"

"No, you can stay. I just didn't want to scare you."

"Can you tell me how she is doing?"

"No ma'am, I cannot because I am not her nurse. You can go out to the nurse's station and they should be able to answer any questions you have."

"Thanks, I will."

I got ready to move and Cam squeezes my hand.

"Oh my God, she's squeezing my hand." I tell her.

"It could be a reflex but let me get her nurse who can contact the doctor."

"Cam, can you hear me?" the doctor keeps asking. "If you can hear me, squeeze my hand."

"Is she waking up?" I ask, nervously.

"Not yet," the doctor replies.

"But I felt her squeeze my hand."

"You may have, and it could have been a reflex or she's telling us that she's fighting, so don't lose hope because we've got to give it time. Her body has been through a lot and it needs time to recover. I'll be back in a little while to check on her."

"Thanks, Dr. Cleaves."

Ray

After visiting Cam, we decide to go to lunch. This may have been a bad decision, after making it to Chili's, in the middle of lunchtime, but thank God we were able to be seated.

I call Anthony while I was in the car to let him know what's going on and that I'd probably need a few days off.

"Has anyone talked to Lyn, this morning? I tried to call but she didn't answer."

"I called too but got her voicemail. I sent her a text, but she hasn't responded," Shelby says, yawning.

"What time did y'all make it home?" I ask.

"Almost six. Man, I can't even begin to imagine what she's going through," Shelby says once we're seated and the waitress gets our drink order.

"Me either. Do they know who the guy is, I mean was?" Chloe asks.

"No, I didn't get a chance to ask her because there

was so much going on last night. Oh, there's something going on with her and Paul, too, because she wouldn't even let him take her to the police station."

"You have any idea what it is?"

"No, but when she's ready, she'll tell us. Speaking of telling us stuff," I say turning to Chloe. "Ma'am, why have you been hiding this baby?"

"Girl, I am just now coming to grips with this pregnancy, myself and telling y'all would make it real."

"Sweetie, newsflash, it is real. There's a whole human growing inside of you."

The waitress returns with our drinks. "Are y'all ready to order?" she asks.

"Not yet, can you give us a few minutes."

"Sure thing. My name is April. Let me know when you're ready."

When she walks off, we turn back to Chloe.

"I know but Lord knows it was a shock to me.

And check this out, I found out on my one-year wedding anniversary," she laughs.

"Girl, so wait, you knew when we were in LA and didn't say nothing?" I scold her.

"Well, I did tell Shelby but, in her defense, she caught me on the elevator and I was deep in thought because this little one has me evaluating everything."

"Like what?"

We all look at Chloe with concern.

"I went to an abortion clinic," she tells us. "Before you say anything, I was too far along to have one, but the fear got the best of me. What if I fail at being a mother?"

"And what if you don't? What are you so afraid of?" Shelby questions. "You've been a great mother to Chris' two daughters, for the last few years."

"I've been step-mother."

"Chloe," I say, taking her hand, "what I've seen with you and those girls, is mothering. There ain't shit step about what you've been to them."

"I agree with Ray," Kerri says. "You're going to be

a great mother, Chloe. However, the biggest question is, have you told Todd? This is Todd's baby, right?"

"Yes, and yes he knows but I wasn't the one who told him. His mom did."

"His mom? You met his mom?"

"No, well yes but let me explain. Todd was in town, for the magazine interview. Taylor reserved this bed and breakfast, in Olive Branch and he decided to cook. Well, let's just say, the smell of the food didn't agree with me and I ended up bolting for the bathroom. Anyway, his mom was there and when I came out the bathroom, she gave me a peppermint and prophesied over the baby, in one breath."

"Whoa."

"Yeah, it was a lot. A little too much for Todd because he said he couldn't handle it and stormed out."

"Oh no, Chloe. What are you going to do?"

She shrugs. "I can't worry about Todd, right now because there are more important things going on."

"Speaking of things," I interject just as the waitress comes to take our food order. We ask for a few more minutes. "Leaving work, the other night, Anthony calls. I meet him at this condo, he'd just purchased and guess who shows up."

"Not his wife?"

"Yes, but it gets better because Justin was with her."

Chloe spits her strawberry lemonade across the table.

"Say what now?"

"Apparently Anthony's wife found out about us and decided to call Justin, so they could confront us together."

"What did Justin say?"

"He tried to act all hurt but I had something for his ass too, when we got home. He's like, Raylan, how long have you been sleeping with your boss," I try to mimic in his voice. "And I say, the same amount of time you've been sleeping with yours."

"WHAT?" Kerri screams causing people to turn

around. "Sorry," she says covering her mouth with her hand.

"Hold up! Isn't Justin's boss a man?" Chloe asks with her hand in the air.

"OH.MY.GOD!" Shelby says. "Ray, I know weren't this calm."

"I was, but that's because I already knew. See," I say pulling out my phone and showing them the video. "He didn't know his boyfriend had sent me this, weeks ago."

"Lord Jesus, I need a shot of whisky." Chloe says with her hand over her heart.

"Heifer, you can't drink."

We all laugh before I continue.

"I knew something was off with him but finding out he's gay, shocked me to my core. Nevertheless, I'll survive because I know, for a fact that I'm a damn good woman."

"You're definitely right about that, but I can't believe Justin," Shelby adds. "Have you been checked out to make sure he hasn't given you anything?"

"I've been tested but it was before all of this. However, it's been months since Justin and I have been intimate."

"This is Lyn, hold on," Shelby says answering her phone. "Hey Lyn, wait, wait slow down. Repeat that. Okay, okay, we're on the way."

"What's wrong?" We're all asking while we watch her grab her purse. "Shelby?"

"Cam, she's waking up."

I throw a $20 bill, on the table, for our drinks as we make a quick exit for the door.

Kerri

"Lyn, what happened? I thought she was waking up?" Shelby asks.

"I thought she was because she squeezed my hand, but Dr. Cleaves said it was just a reflex," she cries as I go over to comfort her, "but I know what I felt."

"It's alright," I tell her. "She'll be awake and causing hell in no time. Cam, girl, we're still here for you, so hurry up and bring your ass back to us. We're not the six pack without you."

"Okay, ladies, visiting time is over," the nurse says, coming to the door, "and we need to take her for another test."

"Before we go, can we all pray together?" Shelby requests.

"God, as we come to you, we first to thank you. Even in the midst of damage and chaos, we thank you. Thank you, God, for being the giver and taker of life but more importantly, we thank you for sparing the lives our sisters.

God, you covered Lyn and she's here and now, we ask that you keep Cam. We don't know what's ahead but we're trusting you. Father, we don't know the plan you have for her, Lyn or for us, but we ask that your will be done.

God, you are protection and peace and although we haven't been faithful, in serving you; forgive us. Forgive us for even thinking we could walk this journey without you. God watch over husbands, children and families and give them strength where they may be weak.

Cover my sister so that she comes out of this temporary situation stronger than she was before. Protect her like only you can and thank you God for keeping each one of us, even in the midst of our mess. God, I submit this prayer to you as if it is already done. Amen."

"Amen. We love you, Cam."

"Are y'all ready to go?" I ask the girls as we're leaving out the room.

"Not yet. Why don't we go to the waiting room and sit for a while?" Lyn suggests.

"I'm going to find a snack machine," Chloe says.

The waiting room is almost empty, by the time we make it there.

"Lyn, how are you?"

She sighs. "I wish I could say I'm okay and meant it but I'm not. My entire world is on fire, literally crumbling before my eyes and I can't do anything about it."

"You've been through something horrific Lyn and you don't have to be strong. What happened to you is going to take some time to heal from."

"It's not just the rape. Paul is having an affair."

"Okay but you knew that, right? I thought y'all decided to put everything behind you and move on."

"I did too but that was before," I pause, "Kandis

decided to show up at my boutique. Oh, that's K-a-n-d-i-s."

"Who is Kandis?" I question.

"Paul's other life."

"Wait, come again." Ray says.

"Apparently, she and Paul have been in a relationship for over three years, they have a son and she came to tell me to divorce him."

We all gasp.

"There's more so hold your wigs, ladies. Kelsey knew about them. And if that wasn't damaging enough, her confession happened, not thirty minutes before I was attacked."

"Lyn, I'm so sorry," Shelby says grabbing my hand. "Is this why you didn't want Paul to go with you?"

I nod.

"Why didn't you tell me last night?"

"Girl, I don't even know how I made it last night, let alone, making it, right now. All I know for sure; my life has hit turbulence and the damages are continuing to be assessed."

"Lyn, you don't have to put up this strong front because we are here for you. If you need a moment to break down, take it and we'll be right here, holding you up," I reassure her.

"I know but I'm scared that if I break, I may not be able to pull myself together. Y'all, I'm so hurt. My neck hurt, my body hurts, my heart hurts and hell, my soul even hurts. It's too much and if I dwell on it, I may not survive it."

"Excuse me," a young lady says. "I don't mean to butt into your conversation, but I overheard what you've said and if you'd allow, I'd like to pray with you all."

"Ma'am, first of all, who are you?" Lyn inquires.

"This is Chaplain Reeves," Shelby says. "She was with Dr. Cleaves, this morning."

"I apologize for interrupting but as I stated, this morning, my name is Chaplain Magnolia Reeves and God wouldn't allow me to leave without offering prayer. I know this isn't normal and I can assure you, I am not crazy, but I have to be obedient and ask."

"Chaplain, who are we to stand in the way of God. Ma'am, you have our permission to pray for out sister, Lyn." Shelby tells her.

"Wait. While you're praying for me, can you please include another prayer for the healing of our sister, Camille who's on a ventilator behind those doors."

"I can do that."

Prayer

"Dear God, before I ask you for anything, I want to first thank you for everything. God, it is because of your power that we can turn this waiting room, into an altar. It is because of you, God, that we can stand before your throne, this afternoon, praying for these sisters.

It is because of your power that we can stop the plans of the enemy, dismantle the attack of sickness, destroy depression and stop suicide. God, without even knowing their plea, you can still deliver and because you can, I can still pray. This is why it doesn't matter where we are because the word says, where two or more are gathered together, touching and agreeing; you'd be in the midst.

Well God, here we are, and we need you. I've read, in your word where you stood at the edge of a grave and gave life to a man who'd been dead four days; surely, you can heal now. I read, in your word, where you healed a woman's daughter and you wasn't even in the same town; surely, you can heal in this place. Your word says, all I have to do is ask, so I'm asking you to shift the atmosphere.

God, you sent me on assignment and here I am. You told me to go and I was obedient. Now, I need you to move. I need you to keep Lyn's mind through the chaos of her storm, quiet the enemy's voice and strengthen her to make it. Father, I don't know what all she's had to endure but I heard her say her world was crashing but I know you can rebuild and restore using the remnants that remain.

Then, don't just stop there because Camille is laid in ICU and she needs to feel your touch. God, I don't know how she got there but I know how she can get out and that's by your power. God, not because you have the power but because you are the power. You are the power of healing, of life and death.

This is why, I'll stand boldly, right here in the midst of this hospital waiting room, declaring healing, deliverance, breakthrough and restoration for all those who stand in need. Do it God. I don't care when or how; I simply need you to do it. Do it for them and for all those who believe.

Strengthen this group of women because they've lost touch with you but now, they're ready to come back to you. God, they got comfortable during the good that they wandered away but you're a forgiving God. Forgive them for their sins and for thinking they could do this without you.

They're home now, God, in you and I trust you to blow their minds. Protect them, provide for them and see them through. We thank you, God and we submit this prayer, on faith knowing you'll do it. Let each of us say, amen."

"Amen," we all say, wiping tears.

Chaplain Reeves begins to speak in tongues.

"I'm sorry," she says as tears spill from her eyes. "There's a reason God is allowing each of you to suffer differently yet at the same time. Please do not curse this test as it'll be what's needed to strengthen you and your faith. Lyn," she says covering her neck, "this wound will leave a scar but do not allow it to be a reminder of what happened. Rather see if for what you survived.

Ladies, I pastor High Point Christian Church and whether you've been there or not, if you all need me, please call. I'm here a few days, per week, as a chaplain or you can join us, for worship on Wednesdays or Sundays. We'd be happy to have you. God bless each of you."

"Wait, what did I miss?" Chloe asks, walking up with an armful of snacks.

Chapter 4

Chloe

"Girl, where have you been?" Ray asks.

"The snack machine didn't have what I wanted so I went to the cafeteria. Why are y'all crying?"

"We just had prayer with Chaplain Reeves," Kerri tells her. "And I don't know how God knew but I'm thankful. Y'all, things have to get better for us, don't they?"

"We have to believe they will," Ray adds. "Like Chaplain Reeves said, it's obvious there's something God wants us to get from this. Why else would He allow each of us to suffer, now?"

"Does it have to be this bad, though?" Lyn asks. "I don't know if I can take anything else."

Shelby is still walking around in circles. Ray goes over to her and we watch as she cries into Ray's arms.

After a few minutes, they come over.

"Y'all, let's get out of here because we need to talk."

We all decide to come back to Shelby's house. Once we're inside, we sit in silence until Shelby begins to speak.

"Isn't it crazy how we can be around each other and still miss out on what's going on? We get so accustomed to seeing each other that we don't take the time to actually see when one of us is hurting. Well, I'm hurting, and I need y'all."

"Shelby, we are here. What is it?"

"Do you all remember me saying, I thought something was going on with Brian, when we were in LA? He has cancer," I say sobbing.

They all surround me.

"What is the doctor saying? Can it be treated?" Lyn inquires once I stop crying.

"I don't know. He has an appointment in two weeks with an oncologist but man, I'd give anything for him to have been cheating."

"Y'all, what's happening with us? A few months ago, we were all happily married, enjoying life—"

"No," Ray interrupts Kerri. "No, we were all pretending. We've gotten good at acting that we forget it isn't real. Now, all hell is breaking loose. It's almost Thanksgiving and I'm having a hard time finding something to be thankful for."

"Are you serious?" I question. "You're healthy, your children are fine, you have a job—"

"I'm also getting a divorce from a man who has been gay most of his damn life."

"So? A divorce isn't the end of the world, Ray because your husband could be sick."

"Hold on Shelby because I didn't mean to upset you. I'm just saying, these last few months have been rough and I don't see the light at the end of the tunnel. Cam is still fighting for her life and Lyn, she's here but she's also fighting. My children's world is being turned upside down and your husband is sick."

"We still have to be thankful," Shelby says. "We have to be."

"We left God," Lyn calmly says, and we turn to her. "There used to be a time, we'd all be in church on

Sunday morning or at bible study on Wednesday but along the way, we stopped."

"We got comfortable," Ray says.

"I agree with that and I can admit, I did. I got comfortable with only offering God the crumbs," Shelby replies. "Now that we're hurting and in pain, He's where we run. I can't even be mad if He doesn't answer because I know for sure, I've been ignoring Him."

"Good thing He doesn't work like that," I tell them. "Look at me. I never thought I'd be divorced and pregnant by a man I barely know. Yet, I am and although I know God doesn't agree with the mess, we get ourselves in, I believe He'll use it to get us to hear His message, whatever it may be."

"Going through this stuff with Justin has me doing a lot of questioning. He told me last night, he only married me because I got pregnant. He's been gay since before we met. His own momma allowed him to cover up who he really was, for all these years because she told him, being gay is a phase. How can a mother honestly tell a child that being gay is a phase without ruining their life?"

"The sad thing Ray, most people don't even understand that. They don't understand how their words and actions can ruin a person's life. It's this kind of stupid mentality that has driven men to live on the down low," Shelby answers.

"Which then causes them to bring AIDS or another STD home to their wife," Kerri adds.

"It's crazy! Now my children's lives are about to be shaken up, all because his momma couldn't deal with the fact her son was, well, is gay. Oh, trust and believe I have a few words for her."

"Wait," Lyn says. "Ray, Justin is gay?"

"Yep."

"And Chloe, you're pregnant by Todd?"

"Are you just now catching that?" I laugh before pulling my shirt back to show her my stomach.

"Girl, I know you are freaking lying!"

I roll my eyes. "I was going to tell y'all,

eventually."

"But you told Todd's, big head ass."

"In my defense, I hadn't planned on telling him either but, now that he knows, he's pissed."

"Can you blame him?" Ray adds. "Judging by the time since Gatlinburg, he's missed half of the pregnancy."

"What was I supposed to tell him, oh hey, I know we had a one-night stand and don't know anything about each other but I'm pregnant and it's yours."

"Yeah," we all say.

"Just how far along are you?" Lyn questions.

"I'll be five months, next week." she smirks. "I'm due February 15th."

"Girl, you need your ass whooped."

We all laugh.

"Well, have you talked to him since?" Kerri asked.

"He sent a text last night, but I wasn't in the right mind frame to deal with him," she replies when her watch dings. "Shoot, I got to go. I have a meeting with my attorney before the divorce hearing. I need to be good and divorced from Chris because in the state of Tennessee, if we're married, he can be added to the birth certificate."

"Yea, you definitely need to get that taken care of. Keep us posted."

"I will and call me with any updates."

Shelby

After everything that happened yesterday, I am looking forward to Bible study tonight. Brian and I, along with the baby, walk into High Point Christian Church.

"Welcome to High Point," a young man says. "Bible Study is getting ready to start in the sanctuary," he tells us, pointing towards the double doors.

"Thank you."

We find seats, toward the back and get settled.

"Good evening High Point. For those of you who are new to High Point, my name is Pastor Magnolia Reeves and we welcome each of you to our weekly bible study. Tonight, we continue with our biblical study on faith and patience.

Turn with me to James one. If you don't have a bible, raise your hands and someone will get you one because we, here at High Point, believe in having access to God's word." She waits before proceeding.

"In James one, verse two through four, it reads; *my brethren, count it all joy when ye fall into divers' temptations; knowing this, that the trying of your faith worketh patience. But let patience have her perfect work, that ye may be perfect and entire, wanting nothing.* Amen."

"Amen," we all say.

"Father God, bless this word on tonight that it will not fall on deaf ears but that your people will be motivated disciples, rightly dividing your word. Amen."

Brian has the baby, so I take my notepad out as Pastor Reeves begins to teach.

"I chose to use the Kings James version of this text, in order for each of us to fully understand the meaning of the words shared. As we discussed on last week, divers, used here, means various and the word temptations signifies affliction, persecution, or trial of any kind.

Patience means endurance. Patience, not in the sense of waiting but in finishing. In verse four, the word perfect doesn't mean without fault but it signifies wholeness or completeness.

Here's what I've learned through many sleepless nights, trials do not produce faith. We're given faith from the abundance of God. For it says, in *Hebrews 11:1*, *"Now faith is the substance of things hoped for, the evidence of things not seen."*

Therefore, this passage is saying is, when trials, persecution, pain, afflictions and etc. show up and we go through them with faith, it produces strength.

Even in this scripture, James is talking to the twelve tribes of Israel who, bible says, are scattered abroad. Yet, he tells them, count it all joy when you fall into diver's temptation. James didn't say if you fall but he says, when you fall because he knows trouble will show up.

It doesn't matter how holy you are, how well you recite scriptures, the amount you pay in tithes or where you sit in church. It also doesn't matter how many Sundays you miss, how many sins you commit, how much alcohol you smoke or weed you drink; trouble is coming.

Beloved, God keeps His promises to us, but the truth is, most of us fail when it comes to the testing of our faith. I used to be ashamed to admit this, but I've been there. See, if my checking account was in the negative, I didn't wait for God to come through, I tried to fix it. If I was in pain, I didn't pray, I tried to fix it.

Why? Because I didn't understand that the test was necessary. I didn't grasp that the trying of my faith was working my strength. All it felt like was, my faith was failing me, and I was failing her. I didn't understand that in order to build my strength, I'd have to be tested.

Then I read James one and specifically verse four that says, but *let patience have her perfect work, that ye may be perfect and entire, wanting nothing.* Here's the thing, God is not requiring us to be perfect, as in flawless but He desires us to be perfect, as in whole.

How many of you know, in order to achieve wholeness, it's going to take some patience as in strength and as in time? See, we think as soon as we say amen, things are supposed to show up, but reality is; it takes patience. And somebody here tonight, your faith is being tested and you're trying to wait but it's hard.

You're in an impossible and tough place and the little bit of hope you had, seems to be dwindling. What do you do? You let patience have her perfect work. This means, you keep going, even though you don't know what's on the other side of your storm. You keep trying God, even though you don't know what the outcome will be.

When you do this, you allow patience to have her perfect work that you may be complete and wanting for nothing. And if you don't know how to do this then verse five and six holds what you've been searching for. It says, *if any of you lack wisdom, let him ask of God, that giveth to all men liberally, and upbraideth not; and it shall be given him. But let him ask in faith, nothing wavering. For he that wavereth is like a wave of the sea driven with the wind and tossed.*

Upbraideth means without reproach or disappointment. I don't know who this lesson is for, on tonight but I do know that when God allows us to go through things, we have to trust the faith He's instilled within us. Whether it's sickness, pain, hurt or whatever; we've all been equipped with the faith to get through it.

And the only way faith can do what you need, you have to first work it. This means doing the surgery man says may not work and allowing this test to build your strength. This means helping folk who talk about you and allowing that test to build your strength. This means standing in the midst of chaos and hell but allowing patience to have her perfect work. Jesus," she exclaims before speaking in tongue.

"I feel a call to pray, right here. I don't know who

this is for and although this is just bible study, God can still move. I know it's Wednesday, but Heaven is still open. Will you stand and join me in prayer? If you need the altar, it's open for you.

Brian and I are both crying as we stand for prayer. A young lady, sitting near us, reaches over and takes Brinae from him, who is still asleep. Brian grabs my hand, leading me to the altar.

Pastor Reeves waits until the altar is filled before she begins to pray.

"Dear God, thank you for not needing my permission to take over this bible study. God, you know the needs of your people and all I desire, is for your will to be done. So, as I stand, and you use my voice, have your way because there's some deliverance that needs to happen, in this place. Have your way because somebody needs healing, tonight.

God, I've lived long enough to know we may not make it to Sunday, so while we have your ear, hear our cries. For the father who simply needs a touch from you, for the mother whose crying has become frequent, for the sister who doesn't know how to tap into their faith and for the brother whose faith is being tested; have your way.

Turn this sanctuary into your operating room, moving the old and creating in us, God, the newness of you. Somebody, in this place, is about to face a storm and their faith is going to be tested. Somebody's family or friend is going through hell, at this moment and their faith is being tested. Somebody is at the end of their rope and their faith is being tested.

Yet, I know you, God, to be the power so I command you to sweep through this place and have your way. Allow the holy spirit to envelop us, like a heavy blanket on a cold night and don't let us go until we feel your presence. Strengthen those who seek it, deliver those who desire it and grant grace to those who feel like giving up.

We thank you Father and we say; it is well with our soul. Let every believer say, amen."

Before Brian and I move, she comes over and lays

her hand on our foreheads, speaking in tongue.

"Try God, trust God and He'll see you through."

Kerri

I make it to the bakery and because I didn't bake yesterday, I am really behind. Kelsey worked this morning and we ran out of everything, so I came in, to prep for Thursday's opening.

MJ is with Michael, who asked to spend some time with him before he leaves for rehab, in the morning.

I look around the kitchen before pulling out all the ingredients I need but then I stop and think about what Shelby told us. It makes me think about a secret, I'm holding, from the girls.

A knock on my office door.

"Hey," I say getting up to give him a hug. "What are you doing here?"

"I need to talk to you about something. The guys working, up front said you were back here."

"Sure, come in and have a seat. What's wrong?"

"I've messed up and I don't know what to do."

"What do you mean, you messed up? Are you cheating? If you are, don't tell me because—"

He holds out some papers. I take the papers and look at them. "Are you freaking serious? Does she know?"

He shakes his head, no.

"They why are you here telling me and not her?" I ask.

"I don't know," he sighs. "You were the first person I thought about, seeing we've been friends since junior high school."

"Mane, we went to the same school for two years before y'all moved to Knoxville. I wouldn't call that friends."

"What about the night we went to the drive-in?" he smiles.

"If you ever repeat that, out loud, again I'll kill you."

"I'm just kidding," he laughs.

"Look, I don't know what advice you're needing, other than, go home and tell your wife."

"I don't know how. This is going to devastate her."

"No, what's going to devastate her, is finding out from someone else. You need to tell her."

"I will," he slinks into the chair. "I just don't know how I let things go this far."

"Look, no matter how far it's gotten, stop it before it gets any farther."

"Just don't tell her, please." He says.

"Do you actually think I'd tell her, now? Hell no, and you better not put me in a position, where I have too, either. She would kill us both."

The delivery bell rings, pulling me from my thoughts. I look through the peep hole to see Adrian.

"One second," I yell washing the flour from my hands before opening the door.

"Hey, what are you doing here?" I ask after allowing him to come in.

"I came by earlier, but the young lady said you had a family emergency. Are you okay? I tried calling, a few times."

"Yeah, I'm fine but who's asking, Adrian or

Bishop?"

"Kerri, I apologize for not telling you, everything about me. I just didn't know how you'd react to knowing, that part of my life."

"No, you knew I wouldn't have slept with you. Let's be real. Adrian, I didn't ask you to tell me everything about your life, but I think, this should have been right up there with, I'm a husband, father and bishop."

"Would that have changed anything? Kerri, I'm still the same person," he tells me. "I'm the person who believes in you and is proud of you. Me wearing a suit and standing in a pulpit doesn't change that."

"It should," I huff, throwing down the towel. "You're a freaking pastor of a church. You lead people, you preach holiness and all that but how can you teach those you serve to get out of sin, if you're still in it? Oh, but you preach really good." I sigh. "Look, I'm not judging you because I have just as much fault, but I've had a rough few days and I'm trying to rebuild my faith. This isn't helping."

"I apologize because you're right." he says. "The bible says in *Romans 14:13*, "*so let's stop condemning each other. Decide instead to live in such a way that you will not cause another believer to stumble and fall.*"

"No, Adrian, this isn't solely on you and that's not what I mean."

"Yea, but I have a deeper responsibility to God's people. I should have been honest, and we never should have crossed that line. Please forgive me."

"I forgive you and please forgive me because truth is, had I not been going through hell, finding out you were a bishop probably wouldn't have mattered. Isn't that crazy?" I question as tears fill my eyes. "A few months ago, I was in a place of craving the attention you gave but from my husband.

I needed to know he was proud of me and when he didn't, you came along. You paid attention and you told me all that I needed to hear."

"That's because I was caught up in my flesh and didn't recognize you were hurting, inwardly. I let you down and for that I'm sorry. I've caused you to stumble and all I can do now, is ask God for forgiveness," he tells me. "Kerri, I do like you and it is my prayer that we get passed this and can remain friends."

I burst into tears and he pulls me into his arms.

"What's wrong? Please tell me."

"It just feels like everything is going wrong. One of my friends is in ICU, another one was attacked, and Michael is leaving for rehab. I don't know how we got here."

He wraps his arms tighter.

"Dear God, I come before your throne, tonight, first asking your forgiveness. Forgive us, oh God, for the sins we've done and for being in flesh. Forgive us, for being outside of your will but thank you for giving us another chance to repent.

Thank you for another opportunity to get it right, in this life. Now, as I stand here with my arms around your daughter, I ask that you hear her cry. Father let her weeping be the prayers, she's yet to speak. Let her tears be the release she needs, to finally come back to you. Let the tears, she shed, be the key to opening the door of her deliverance.

God, as we stand here, arm in arm, I ask that you move me out the way and let her feel you. God, for it's you she needs. Not just for her but for the friends who are also going through. Even, God, bless her husband, on his journey to being healed. We know that you are a God of infinite chances, you are a God who can heal, you are a God who can deliver, and you are a God who forgives.

Thank you, Father. Before our prayers are ended, thank you. Before you do what only you can, thank you. Before you even release it to be so, thank you. For I know that if we ask, you'll do it. Thank you, God and amen."

"Amen," I say as a whisper.

He releases me, and I grab the towel from the counter.

"Thank you, Adrian. I really needed that and

even though I was being sarcastic earlier, you really can preach."

"Thank you. And I meant what I said. I would like to remain friends with you."

"I don't know about that."

"Why not? Do you not trust me?"

"It's not that but I got the feeling, your wife doesn't like me. Not that I care but I don't need those problems."

"What do you mean?"

"That night at the church, she came up and introduced herself, in a nice and nasty kind of way. She wouldn't even shake my hand," I laugh. "She said something about knowing how you are around women and she expects our relationship to be just business. I told her if it was going to be a problem, before it began, no need to continue on."

"Wow, she made it seem like you were the one who was nasty."

"Adrian, I didn't have a reason to be nasty to that

lady. Hell, I didn't even know who she was. Anyway, I don't mind honoring the contract, if there's still going to be one but I will not fight with her."

"Yes, I still want your pastries in my store and I can promise you there will be no problem," he states.

"Good, then send me the contract and I will have a lawyer look over it."

"Will do but it looks like you're in for a long night. Anything I can help with?"

"You sure?"

"Yeah, I can put flour in a bowl."

"Then here," I say throwing him an apron, "because I could surely use the help."

Ray

After everything that's been going on, I decided to take the day off and spend it with the kids. They boys have been questioning why Justin hasn't been home and although they've tried to call him a few times, he hasn't answered.

Rashida is still processing the news, she heard from, her dad, the other night and she'd been very quiet and withdrawn.

The boys are trying to figure out what's going on, but I haven't gone into detail yet because the biggest part of it, Justin would have to do himself.

Pulling up, at the house, I roll my eyes when I see Justin's truck in the garage. His trunk is up, and he has some boxes in the back.

"What's dad doing?" Tristan questions.

Before I could get the truck in park, they jump out.

"Dad, what's going on? Why are you moving boxes?" JJ questions.

"And where have you been?" JJ asks. "We've been calling you. Why didn't you answer?"

"Guys, I'll explain everything once we get inside."

I ask the kids to leave their bags, by the door and come into the den. Justin is pacing and looking like he's about to be sick. Although I didn't like his ass very much, I feel sorry for him but more than anything, I'm worried for the kids.

Their entire life is about to change and there is nothing I can do about it. I only pray this doesn't change their feelings toward him because he is a great dad.

"I don't know why you're pacing, you may as well tell them the truth," Rashida barks.

"The truth about what?" Tristan asks.

"Your pappy is gay, and I don't mean the happy kind."

"Rashida, that's enough. Sit down and let your

dad talk."

"You're lying," JJ screams. "Dad, tell her, she's lying."

"JJ, I'm sorry but I can't do that. I am gay, but you have to know I love all of you and this doesn't change anything. I'm still your dad."

"What the hell do you mean?" Rashida responds with an attitude and her hands balled into fists. "This does change everything. You're gay."

"I'm still your dad," Justin cries.

"You're still our dad who likes to sleep with other men. This is so messed up," JJ yells, knocking a picture off the table.

"JJ and Rashida, stop! I know this is a lot to take in and you have every right to be upset but the cursing and breaking things ends, now. Sit down and let your dad finish." I walk over to Tristan who hasn't said anything yet.

"What could he possibly say to top this?" Rashida asks.

"Rashida, I'm sorry and I never intended to hurt any of you. You all are my life," Justin says still crying, "and I cannot live without you. All I'm asking for is time to figure this out and forgiveness."

"Mom, did you know?" Tristan asks, looking at me with tears in his eyes. I shake my head, no. "Does this mean y'all are getting divorced?"

"Yes," I answer.

"I hate you!" Tristan yells at Justin before running to his room.

"How long?" Rashida questions. "How long have you been gay?"

"Rashida, baby, we can discuss that later—"

"No, mom, we're not babies anymore, and we deserve to know. I'll be seventeen soon and don't want to be treated like a child. Answer the question, Dad."

"Since I was about 14. I told my mom when I was 16," he answers.

"Wait, grandma knows you're gay?" JJ questions with a shocked expression.

"Yes," he says wiping his face. "I never told anyone else and neither did she."

"Rashida and JJ, go to your rooms."

"I'm glad you're moving out because we all deserve better than this." Rashida says grabbing JJ and leaving the room.

I wait until they're gone.

"Raylan, I cannot lose my family."

"What did you think would happen, Justin? You're gay and have been our entire marriage."

"I've never acted on it, though."

"Should I be grateful? The fact still remains, you don't love me."

"I do love you."

"Not like a husband should. You've grown to love me, as the mother of your children, the one who kept your house and washed your clothes, but you've never loved me, loved me. Hell, come to think of it, all I was to you was a maid with occasional sex. Humph, go figure."

"Ray, it wasn't like that."

"No, then tell me I'm wrong. You said yourself, the only reason you married me was because I was pregnant and the only reason you've stayed is because you knocked me up, three more times. This isn't love and I agree with Rashida, we deserve better."

"Since coming out to my mother, she tried everything in her power to change me. She said it was a phase and that I'd eventually grow out of it. She even sent me to some camp that was supposed to scare me straight and it worked, for a while," he adds.

"Am I supposed to feel sorry for you? Boo, you've been in your right mind, this entire time and it had nothing to do with your mother. You are a grown man, capable of deciding how you wanted to live your life. Instead, you settled, to appease your mother."

"I didn't mean to hurt y'all."

"Dude, how could you not think this would hurt them or me, for that matter? Justin, you're gay and have been gay, your entire freaking life. Have you been cheating our entire marriage?"

"No! Ray, I promise this was the only time. I suppressed those feelings—"

"Until Travis." I say, finishing his sentence. "Did you ever sleep with the both of us?"

"No but Ray, I'm willing to stop seeing him if you take me back. I'll get tested and go to therapy or whatever it takes because I want my family," he says, walking over to me.

"Your family? You actually think I would take you back, as my husband, knowing you're gay and sleeping with a man?"

"You've been sleeping with a man and I'm willing to forgive you. Why can't you forgive me?"

"Pooh, I'm supposed to sleep with men because that's how God designed it. However, let me make this clear to you," I say walking closer to him. "There will never be a 'us' again because if Travis was able to wake up those feelings, after all these years, they won't be suppressed again."

"I can do it."

"Well, do it with somebody else because I refuse to settle for anything less than what I know I deserve and I damn sure won't compete with a man. You made your choice, so deal with it. Yes, I made a mistake by cheating on you, but that's because you didn't want what I had to offer anyway."

"I don't want to lose my kids, Raylan."

My phone vibrates with a call.

"Then you need to figure out a way to get them to forgive you but as for me, I'm all the way done." I tell him before answering the phone and walking out.

Lyn

"Ah," he grunts, slapping my butt over and over. "I may have to get this again. Ah, how'd you like that big baby?" he taunts.

"I may have to get this again, big baby. Did you hear me? I may have to get this again."

I jump up, swinging before my eyes focus and I realize, I'm in my bedroom. I sit up on the side of the bed, reaching into the nightstand drawer for the sleeping pills. I slam the drawer short when I remember throwing the out.

"Mom," Kelsey knocks on the door. "Mom," she says again.

"Not now."

She pushes the door open anyway.

"I only came to see how you're feeling? Dad told me what happened. Are you okay?"

"No, and I don't want to talk about it," I state. "Close the door on your way out."

"Mom, please," she breaks down crying. "I'm sorry you had to find out about Ms. Kandis, like this. I never meant to hurt you."

"Ms. Kandis," I repeat, dryly. "Well, it seems Ms. Kandis was the only one who had the decency to finally tell me the truth."

"I didn't know how."

"Are you serious? Mom, dad's having an affair. You see how easy that was? The words just roll off your tongue."

"But it wasn't my place."

This time I chuckle. "Oh, but your place was at her house, with her son while y'all laughed and ate dinner and went on vacations? Got it."

"That's not what I meant," she says, wiping tears."

"That's exactly what you meant because you and your father have kept this secret, for however long it was. Now, you can keep your tears and apology." I get out of bed and walk into the bathroom, slamming the door.

After taking a shower and changing the bandage, on my neck; I open the door to Paul sitting at the edge of the bed.

"Whatever it is, you want to say, don't because I'm not in the mood or right frame of mind."

"Lyn don't take your anger out on Kelsey," he states.

"Don't tell me what in the hell to do. You and her both lied to me."

"All of this is on me," he clarifies

"No, this is on the both of you. Kelsey is seventeen years old and she knows right from wrong. Let me ask you a question. Do you have any idea how embarrassing it was to not only find out, my husband has been having an affair for years, has a whole other family but that my daughter supports it?"

"It wasn't like that," Kelsey cries from the door. "I didn't want to hurt you."

"That's bullshit!" I yell, grabbing my neck and breathing. "Stop trying to pacify the situation. You were both wrong," I say starting to cry. "You both did this."

When Kelsey walks toward me, I put up my hand.

"No," I shake my head. "I don't want your pity because neither of you thought enough of me not to cause this pain. What I can't figure out is why, though. I know I'm not perfect, but I never expected this. What did I do to deserve this?"

Kelsey is crying.

"Lyn, I get that you're mad, but eventually we will have to deal with this, so don't shut us out. You've been through a lot—"

"You think?"

"Mom, please," Kelsey cries and Paul stands up to console her.

"Babe, please let us be here for you," he whines.

"Nah, I'll pass. I don't want either of you anywhere near me because if this is the kind of love you have to offer, keep it."

"We do love you."

I throw a bottle of perfume into the wall. "This isn't love! Do you have any idea how much this hurts? It hurts more than what that man did to me that night. What hurts even more, had you been there, this probably wouldn't have happened. But again, I was put on the back burner because you had to go and take care of Kandis."

"Lyn, I fucked up and I'm sorry for the way I've handled all of this. I never should have left you; I never should have put Kelsey in my mess, I never should have had the affair—"

"You never should have had another baby, you never should have made a home with your mistress— yea, the list goes on and on. However, the fact remains, you did all those things. Not for a few months but for years. FREAKING YEARS! Everything we've had has been a lie."

"Lyn, all I'm asking is, please don't take this out

on Kelsey."

"What am I supposed to do, Paul? Just forget all this and wrap her in my arms? Am I supposed to wipe the tears of guilt? NO.THANK.YOU! Now, please just leave me alone because right now, I'm tired, mentally more than physically and the next time I ask, either of you to leave; it won't be this nice."

"I'm sorry," they say at the same time.

"So am I because now, I have to reevaluate everything and until I do, I'm not at a place of forgiveness."

Chapter 5

Lyn

"Please stop!"

"Now you beg," he laughs. "I'll stop when you quit fighting because I'm getting what I came here for. Next time, you'll stop being a tease and you'll think before trying to get me fired."

"Okay, I won't fight but please stop pulling my hair."

Laughing. More laughing.

"If you move, I'll split your throat and if you need to know that I'm not playing."

Laughing. "Stab her Xavier! Stab her now!"

"Shut up Kandis, I got this."

I jump up, grabbing my neck. My tank top is stuck to me, from sweating. Looking around, I see that I'm on the couch in the living room.

I swing my legs over the edge and put my head in my hands. When I finally stand, I see pictures of times when I thought we were happy. I go over to the mantle and after lingering there, I swipe all of the pictures into the floor and scream.

Paul comes running into the living room.

I take the fireplace poker and begin hitting the TV while still screaming.

"Lyn, baby, stop."

"Leave me alone! You did this!"

"I know," he pleads, "I know but you're bleeding."

When he takes a step towards me, I hold out the poker. "Don't."

"Please Lyn. Just let me help you."

"Help me?" I boil with anger before busting the glass out of the coffee table.

"Where were you when that man was raping me?"

I break more glass. "Where were you when Kandis was laughing at me?" I break more glass. "Where was your help when he was cutting my throat? When I needed you, where were you?"

I start to stagger and bump into the wall.

"Mom," Kelsey cries.

"Mom," I mock. "I don't want your help either," I slur. "Just leave me alone."

I drop the poker and slide down to the floor. When I see the blood, turning my shirt red, I wipe my hand across it and laugh. "I guess you can tell your girlfriend she was right about me being unstable."

"Kelsey, call 911," is the last thing I hear Paul say.

*****

I open my eyes.

"Lyn?"

"Where am I? Ah," I moan.

"You're in the hospital. You busted your stitches and lost a lot of blood."

I squeeze my eyes shut and when I try to move my hands, I can't.

"What the hell?"

"They had to restrain you because you kept fighting," Paul says.

"And you let them?"

"I didn't have a choice, or you would have bled to death."

"Maybe you should have let me. Now, untie these freaking things."

When he does, I rub my wrists before raising the bed to sit up.

"Why are you here Paul?"

"Because you're my wife and I'm worried about you," he tells me.

"Don't be."

"Lyn, I know I hurt you and I'm sorry, but will you at least let me help you through this."

"This? You say it like I had wisdom teeth pulled. Paul, had you come back to talk to me, that day, instead of chasing Kandis, I wouldn't have gotten raped."

"Do you have any idea, how many times I've replayed that day in my head? Yes, I should have been there. Yes, I let you down again and I'm sorry."

"Well, sorry doesn't stop my nightmares."

"What can I do?"

"You can leave."

"I'm not leaving you and what did you mean by tell my girlfriend she was right?"

"About me being unstable. Isn't that what you told her, that I was crazy?"

"No—"

A knock on the door stops him.

"Good afternoon, my name is Rev. Denise French and I'm one of the onsite chaplains. You're Mrs. Williams?"

"Yes ma'am, but I'm really not in the mood for your chaplain services."

"Lyn, you don't have to be rude," Paul says.

"And you don't have to be here," I shoot back.

"Mrs. Williams, I apologize if my stopping by is upsetting you. I only wanted to drop off my card and offer prayer, but I can come back."

"Can your prayer change time? If so, then take me back to 2015, before my husband had an affair with a woman who bore him a son. Can you pray for that? If not, then I'm not interested."

"If I did have the power to change time, I wouldn't because changing time won't change our circumstances. It may delay them, but it will not destroy them. Mrs. Williams, we're all appointed a time of suffering. Sure, some things are caused by our fleshly desires, but others are tied to our destiny. Who are we to stop God's plan for our life?"

"God's plan? Was God's plan for me to be raped?"

"No, that's a part of evil's plan. God's plan was for you to survive."

"Survive?" I laugh. "This isn't surviving, Rev. French because every time I close my eyes, I see that evil. Every time I take a deep breath, I feel that evil and every time I look in the mirror; I'm reminded of what evil did to me. This isn't surviving."

"Lyn—"

"Paul shut the hell up. As a matter of fact, leave and take Rev. French with you."

I lower the bed and turn over.

"I'll leave my card and when you're ready, call me."

Shelby

I wake up to Brian smiling at me.

"What are you smiling about?" I ask him.

"Nothing, I was just watching you sleep."

"Well, that's creepy but good morning."

"I've missed you," he says, rubbing my face. "I've missed this."

"Yea, yea! I hear you."

"Oh, so that's all I get after telling you that?" he asks, tickling me.

"Stop, stop! I'm sorry."

"You will be sorry when I'm done," he tells me, rolling on top of me.

He kisses me on my lips, moves to my neck, my breasts, my stomach and— "No, I haven't showered yet."

He pushes my hands away as his mouth moves lower. I moan my pleasure, "oh, that feels so good!"

"Now this is what I missed," I smile when he rolls off of me. "You're going to be late for work."

"Yea, but it was well worth it," he says laying down.

"What time is your doctor's appointment, next week?"

"3:30, to discuss the results of the MRI."

"How are you feeling about all of this?" I inquire, laying my head on his chest.

"I honestly don't know, babe. I've tried to do a little research and a whole lot of praying but I don't know. All I can do is exactly what Pastor Reeves said."

"Try God, trust God and He'll see us through," we both say together.

"It's all I can do, at the moment. So, I'm going to trust God to see me through. And thank you."

"For what?"

"For getting me to go back to church. If Sunday worship is anything like bible study, I cannot wait to go."

"Me either. I really enjoyed it, but would you be upset if I've reached out to Pastor Reeves for prayer?"

"Of course not. We can use all the prayer, we can get," he says kissing the top of my head.

"Amen to that and know that I am here for you, no matter what you face, we will face it together," I say. "Do you want breakfast before you go?"

"Nah, because I'm not going into the office. Let's stay here for a while then do lunch."

I raise up to look at him. "Really?"

He nods.

"Then you have me until I go to visit with Cam, later."

"I'll go with you."

"Cool," I say snuggling up to him.

"I love you Shelby and I don't know what I would do without you."

"I love you too and I know you're going to be fine," I say, kissing him.

We both fall asleep and by the time the baby wakes us, it's 11 AM.

"I'll get her if you want to go ahead and shower," I tell Brian. "I'm sure she's hungry and wet because she normally doesn't sleep this long."

"Okay. I'll come and get her once I'm done."

By the time we leave the house, it's after three. We drop Brinae off at Mrs. Gray's and decide on a sushi restaurant not far from the hospital. After we're seated and placed our order, Brian grabs my hand.

"Babe, we need a vacation," I tell him.

"I agree and now that Brinae is old enough, I think we should take one. Where do you want to go?"

"I don't know but it will be somewhere hot."

"Then plan it, wherever you want."

"Do you want to wait until after your doctor's appointment? We don't know what type of treatment plan you'll be on." I ask.

"That's why I want to do it before treatment

because I don't know what all that will entail and if this happens to be my last vacation with you and our daughter, I want to enjoy it, fully."

"Brian don't talk like that. We have to believe and have faith that you're going to beat this."

"Babe, we also have to be realistic and just in case I don't, I want to enjoy the moments we have left."

I sigh, trying to keep my emotions in check as the waitress sits our drinks down.

"Shelby, look at me," Brian says. "You know I love you, right?"

"Of course. Through sickness and in health. I hope you know that."

He kisses the back of my hand. "I do."

An hour later, we walk through the doors of the ICU but when we get to Cam's door, there are nurses surrounding her bed and it looks like she's struggling.

"Oh God," I say covering my chest with my hand. "Cam, please be alright."

Cam

I open my eyes and my surroundings are unfamiliar. "Courtney," flashes in my mind. I try to move but my body hurts. I try to speak but there's something in my mouth. I reach for it, but I can't get it out. I start to freak out, my heart starts to beat faster and there's a beeping sound.

I jump when a woman tower over me.

"Mrs. Shannon, calm down. Mrs. Shannon, can you hear me? Page Dr. Cleaves and respiratory because she's awake."

I continue to fight, internally screaming.

"Where am I? Please tell me. Why can't anybody hear me?"

"Mrs. Shannon, I need you to calm down or I will need to give you something to sedate you."

"Cam, please," I hear Shelby say. "Sister, please listen to the nurse and stop fighting. I'm here and you're not alone."

I stop.

"Shelby?" I hear her, but I don't see her.

"Mrs. Shannon, I know you may be confused but I need you to listen. My name is Theodora and I'm here to help you. Do you understand?"

I shake my head yes.

"Good."

She goes over to the machine and I turn my head to see Shelby and Brian, standing in the hallway. I feel the tears running down the side of my face.

A few minutes later, a man and another woman rush in.

"Is she fully awake?"

"Yes, doctor."

"What about her vitals?"

"All good."

"Great. Mrs. Shannon, my name is Dr. Cleaves. Do you know where you are?"

I shake my head, no.

"You're in the hospital but you're going to be

okay. You've been asleep for a few days and right now, we're happy to have you with us but I need you to calm down and listen."

I nod.

"Good. Can you squeeze my hands?"

I do.

"Good. Are you in pain?"

I shake my head no.

"Good." He turns to look at the machine beside me before talking to the nurse and the other lady. He turns back to me. "You have a tube, in your throat that has been helping you breathe and giving your heart time to recover from the trauma, you've experienced."

"Trauma?" I think, confused.

"I will explain once I get this tube out"

I nod.

"I'm going to need you to help me. Can you do that?"

I nod.

"Okay. Nurse Theodora along with Tara, from

respiratory is going to assist me. Ladies, are you ready?"

They both reply.

"Okay, Mrs. Shannon. First, Tara is going to suction your mouth and throat. When she's done, I'm going to ask you to cough, a few times just to make sure we get all the fluid that may be in your mouth. The final time, I'll ask is when I'll remove the tube to make you more comfortable. Do you understand?"

I nod, yes. Theodora begins to remove the tape from my face.

"Okay, cough for me and one more time. Good," he says as the lady sticks something into my mouth.

"You're doing good."

She sticks the thing into my mouth again before motioning to the doctor.

"This time, when you cough, I'm going to withdraw the tube. Please don't reach for the tube and be as still as possible," Dr. Cleaves says. "Now, cough. Good."

Tara places an oxygen mask over my face and does more suction. Once she's done, I've never been so happy to take a deep breath.

Theodora hands me a cup of water. "Sip this slow," she instructs. "You've had a tube down your throat so it's going to be sore."

I wince as the water goes down.

"Where's Courtney?" I whisper.

Dr. Cleaves looks at Shelby.

"Cam, I've called Thomas and I'm sure she's on the way with him."

"So, she's okay?"

"Yes, why wouldn't she be?"

I start to cry before lowering the mask again, "what happened to me?" I cringe from the burning of my throat.

"Would you like to wait until your husband arrives?"

I shake my head, no.

"You experienced what we call, cocaine toxicity. Whenever cocaine, in large amounts, are ingested, it activates your central nervous system. Cocaine is a drug that excite neurotransmitters, in the brain. Due to this, we sedated you and placed you on life support."

"Oh God," I cry, grabbing my throat. "Am I going to be okay?"

"Yes, but Mrs. Shannon, your body went into shock and for a while, you were in grave danger. I have to tell you, you're very blessed because not a lot of people survive the state you were in. You should be very grateful."

As he speaks, I cry.

"I'm going to order a few tests, to ensure there are no residual damage—"

"Damage?" I whisper.

"Listen, I know this is a lot to take in, but you've experienced two seizures, since you've been here. I have to make sure there are no underlying issues so, we will need to run tests to check your organ function. I'll be back in a moment."

"What have I done?" I cry, when he leaves.

"Cam," Shelby says coming over to me. "I'm so happy to see you awake."

"Shelby, what did I do?"

"You made a mistake but you're alive," she tells me. "I've already called Thomas, but I need to call the girls. I'll be right back."

I grab her hand. "Wait," I whisper. "I'm sorry."

"All of that can wait, you're awake and that's all that matters."

While she's gone, Theodora and another nurse comes to get blood and some of my urine, from the catheter. When they leave, I close my eyes and cry.

"Cam, why are you crying? Are you hurting?" Shelby asks when she comes back.

I shake my head. "I was so stupid. How could I have been so stupid."

She sighs before sitting on the bed. "You weren't thinking but the blessing is, you made it. Everything else can be worked out, if you want it to be."

"How long have I been here?" I whisper.

"Since Monday."

"And what day is it?"

"Monday, the following week."

"Do you remember anything that happened or why you weren't at home?"

I shake my head, no and cry harder. She sits next to the bed, pulling me into her.

When I release her, I look up to see Thomas and my children.

"Thomas, I'm so sorry."

Chloe

Walking into the court house, I am met by my attorney, Abigail Alston.

"Hey Chloe, we should be called into the courtroom, within thirty minutes. Do you have any questions before we go before the judge?"

"Nope, none that I can think of."

"Great. As I told you, when we spoke a few days ago, this is just a formality. We didn't necessarily have to have a hearing but then you'd have to wait to get the judgment, in the mail. This way, the judge can grant the divorce and it'll be over."

"I understand and thank you for pushing the paperwork through. The faster I get this done, the better."

"I hear that. I have all the paperwork you'll need but the judge will ask some questions, to ensure everything we've agreed on, is what you want."

Both of our phone vibrates at the same time. She

nods and walks off. I open my messages to a text from Todd, asking if we can meet today. I send him a response, put my phone on silent and into my purse.

I look up to see Chris headed my way. I make sure my shirt isn't clinging to my stomach as I move my purse in front of me.

"Hey," he says.

"What's up Chris?"

"Dang, it's like that? I just came over to speak while you're still Mrs. Chris Lark."

"Hey, hello and goodbye."

I turn to walk off.

"Wait," he says. "I want to ask you something."

I roll my eyes and turn back to him. He steps closer, to whisper.

"Chloe, I know we've already agreed to everything and the paperwork is filed, but I was hoping you'd let me borrow some money."

I open my mouth to cuss his ass out, but my saliva goes down wrong and I start coughing. I hold up the one finger, while I go over to the water fountain. I dislike drinking from them, but I needed something, quick.

"You okay?" he questions.

"Yea, but you must not be."

"What do you mean?"

"Chloe," Abigail calls out, "we're ready."

"Wait," Chris says but I keep walking.

Inside the courtroom, we are sworn in as we stand before the judge. I sit my purse on the table, in front of me and he gets right to business.

"State your names," the judge sternly says.

I look at Abigail and she nods.

"Chloe Lark."

"Chris Lark."

The judge is flipping through papers. "Were you both a resident of Tennessee for six months, immediately before you filed for divorce?"

"Yes," we state.

"Have both parties entered into a Marital Dissolution Agreement that fairly and equitably divides your assets and debts?"

"Yes."

"Do you share any biological children?" he inquires, looking from me to Chris.

"No, your honor."

"Mr. Lark, did you give your spouse notice regarding continuing health insurance coverage?"

"No, your honor," his attorney speaks. "They both have their own insurance plans."

"Is that true, Mrs. Lark?" the judge asks.

"Yes, your honor."

"As part of your agreement, will you each be covering your own court costs?"

"Yes, honor."

"And are you asking the court to grant you a divorce on the ground of irreconcilable differences?"

"Yes, your honor."

"Very well. According to the Marital Dissolution Agreement, before me, both of you have agreed to the following. There will be no spousal support paid by either of you. Mrs. Lark will retain the home and car, she owned prior to the marriage. Mr. Lark will retain ownership of his car and all belongings he bought into the marriage.

There will be no division of any 401K or other financial bank accounts, individually owned by each party. Mrs. Lark has asked for some sort of visitation with Lauren and Brittney, the biological children of Mr. Lark; that will be agreed upon outside of this divorce decree. Is that correct?" he asks us.

"That's correct," I say.

"That's correct," Chris adds. "And I have no problem with her staying in the girl's life."

"Is there anything else?"

"No, your honor," my attorney says.

"Hold on," Chris says. "What about her business?"

"What about it?" I ask.

"Don't I get something from it?"

I laugh, so does my attorney and the judge hit the gavel.

"Your honor, Mrs. Lark's business, Truth Magazine was founded before she and Mr. Lark were married, and he never said anything about it, until now," my attorney corrects.

"Well, I'm saying something now." Chris states. "Your honor, I have a new baby on the way and—"

"You're pregnant?" the judge asks me. "I specifically asked if there were any biological children."

"Your honor, he isn't talking about me. He's referring to his ex-wife."

"Sir, your ex-wife is pregnant by you, while you're standing here getting divorced from your current wife and you want me to do what, exactly?"

"All I'm asking for is about $10,000. She has the money."

"And sense with it," I say, and Abigail grabs my arm.

"Mrs. Lark, I'm incline to agree with you. Mr. Lark, you signed an agreement where it states what you wanted with this divorce and sir, that was nothing. Who am I to change that? This divorce is granted." He hits the gavel. "Next case."

"That's it?" I ask Abigail.

"Yep, you are officially divorced. You will get the papers in the mail but that's it."

"Thank you, Jesus," I exclaim, giving her a hug and hurrying out of the courtroom.

"Chloe?"

I keep walking until I get to the elevator.

"Chloe? I know you hear me."

"Man, what?"

"Can't you help me out?"

"Yes, help your ass right out of my face. Dude, you have some nerve asking me for money, after all the damaged you've caused. I built that company and I'll be damned if I allow you to take one penny from it, especially one you'll use to take care of you and your cheating ass ex-wife. Now, goodbye, for good."

"What about the girls?"

I stop in my tracks. "What about them?"

"You want some sort of agreement to see them, don't you? Well, it'll cost you."

I laugh. "As much as I love those girls, I'm still not willing to pay you a dime. And knowing you'd willingly try to blackmail me, using them, makes me thank God, I never had a baby by you. You're a disgusting waste of human flesh and I hope God repays you, every ounce of what you're due."

I step on the elevator and throw him the middle finger before the door closes and my phone rings.

"What's up Shelby?"

Ray

"Good morning Ray, I've already loaded your schedule to your tablet but here's a printed copy."

"Thanks, has Mr. Johnson made it in yet?"

"No, he called to say he may not be in today and needs you to handle the staff meeting, this afternoon. He's sending you some information via email. I've also sent the final counts for the company's Thanksgiving dinner, next month."

"Thanks, I'll take care of it."

"Oh, last thing," she says. "Mr. Johnson wanted you to approve the budget for the Christmas party, too. I also sent it."

"Anything else, boss lady?"

She laughs, "no ma'am but if there is, I'll buzz you."

"Thanks, and please hold my calls for the next

hour so I can get through some of this."

"Sure thing. If you need anything in the meantime, let me know," she says before I close the door.

Twenty minutes later, Shelly buzzes.

"What's up Shelly?"

"Um, Mr. Johnson's wife is here to see you. I told her you didn't want to be disturbed but she won't take no for an answer," she whispers.

"Send her in."

I push the laptop back on my desk as she walks in. She looks around.

"Kris, what can I do for you?" I ask as she closes the door. "Anthony is not here."

"I know and good morning to you too, can I sit?"

"Sure."

"I'm going to get right to it. I'm not giving you my husband."

"Uh, ma'am, you can't give me anything I'm not interested in having nor did I ask for. Furthermore,

Anthony isn't a piece of property, he's a grown man and the last I checked, he was capable of making decisions on his own."

"Not when you're influencing him. Before you came along, we didn't have any problems and now he's ready to divorce me. Well I'll be damned if that's going to happen. I've invested too many years to watch you take it away."

"Listen Linda," I say sighing loudly, "I am not to blame for whatever problems are happening in your household. If I were a betting woman, I'd bet my entire next paycheck that you were having issues, long before me and if you think I'm about to be the scapegoat, think again."

"You are the reason. Anthony has never cheated on me, before you, because I do everything for him. You came along, making it easy for him to break his vows because you're right here, in his face."

"Girl, Anthony hasn't cheated, that you know of. However, let me make something perfectly clear. There's nothing easy about me. I've worked at this company for over seven years and we've never crossed that line, until a few months ago. I'm sorry that it happened but it did, and we can't change that.

But just so you know, you can give a man the best sex, every kind of way; cook the best meals, dress up in lingerie seventeen times, in seven days, fry bacon in the nude and shave every piece of hair from your body; if that's what your man wants and he'll still cheat."

"That's not true. Women like you, are the reason men like my Anthony cheats. You'll do whatever he asks, making it hard for me to satisfy him."

"Did you not just hear what I said? Kris, if you think for one moment, sex is what Anthony was after, you're delusional. The only thing I gave Anthony, that you haven't is attention and it's the same thing he gave me. Sex, anybody can do that."

"Attention? He's not a child or a puppy. He's a grown man who knows my daily responsibilities. I raise our daughter and run fundraisers for the charities, he loves. He doesn't want a housekeeper, so I have to clean the house and then he expects me to cook dinner. With the money he makes, I should have a chef, nanny, and a housekeeper."

"Wow. You sound like a great helper but when are you wife, friend, confidant, prayer partner, back rubber and everything else he needs?"

"I don't have time for that," she says, waving her hand.

"Yea, well, you might not but the next woman who is trying to become Mrs. Anthony Johnson does and believe me, it isn't me."

She looks at me.

"When was the last time you sat down and had a real conversation without tracking his phone, looking through his emails, calling numbers you find on the cell phone bill or acting plum silly? When was the last time you treated him like he was grown?"

She starts to cry.

"Kris, you want me to be the reason because I'm right here as something tangible, you can see and it's easier to blame me. However, I'm not the problem, sweetie. Maybe you should take a look at yourself."

"I'm sorry for coming here. I just don't want to lose my husband. He's been my everything since I met him."

"First, that's your problem. Girl, a man can't be your everything. I don't care how good he looks, how much money he makes or how good he makes you feel. You have to love you, otherwise, you'll feel like you have nothing else to live for, when he's ready to call it quits. Second, what are you to you?"

"What do you mean?" she asks sniffling.

"If he's your everything, where do you fit in? Baby, you have to put you first, sometime because if you don't, you'll lose your identity. You'll be so wrapped up in him that you'll forget who you are. When this happens, you'll find yourself confronting a woman who has nothing to do with the issues that were there, before her."

"What do I do?"

"Find a therapist," I say standing up. "Kris, I'm sorry for what happened between Anthony and I because it was a mistake but the underlying issues, have to be fixed. You're a beautiful woman who needs to know that."

She stands, and I walk around the desk.

"Thank you Raylan and I'm sorry, again for coming here."

She leaves out and Shelly comes to the door.

"Is she okay?" she asks.

"I hope she will be."

*****

"In closing, I, on behalf of Mr. Johnson, would like to thank everyone for a great quarter. I know we've been extremely busy these last few months and I appreciate all the efforts you've played in finalizing this last merger. As of last week, I am happy to say it has closed and everything worked out in our favor."

Everyone claps.

"As a way to say thank you, Mr. Johnson has approved, next week, as our first official, fall break."

Everyone cheers.

"If there's nothing more, this concludes our meeting and if I don't see you before next week, have a great vacation."

I wait until everyone is gone before I gather my things. I look up and Anthony is standing at the door.

"Hey, are you okay?"

"No but thank you for handling the meeting. I tried to get back in time."

"It's cool but are you sure, everything is okay?"

He sits in one of the chairs.

"Anthony, what's going on?"

"Nothing, I'm just tired. Kris is making this divorce so much harder than it has to be. Every freaking hour, she's calling to argue."

"Speaking of Kris, she came to see me."

"You're kidding?" he blows. "Raylan, I apologize because I shouldn't have drug you into my mess."

"Anthony, what happened between us was a mistake, but I will not lie and say, it wasn't what I needed at the time. However, I've had enough drama in my life, these last few months, to last a lifetime. Kris doesn't seem like a bad person, but she doesn't know who she is. Her entire life is wrapped up in you."

"I know, and she's always been that way. I've tried to get her to start a business or at least a hobby but she won't. All she does, is look through my phone and do crazy stuff."

"Well, you'd better get her some help."

"Nah, I'm going to give her a divorce. I've already started the process."

"Good luck with that," I tell him when I see the text from Shelby. "I have to go, Cam is awake."

Chapter 6

Lyn

Since my redecorating of the house, the other day, I was released from the hospital, but I didn't go home. I haven't talked to Paul and I hope he didn't say anything to the girls because I'm not ready to deal with their pity.

After an early morning doctor's appointment, to check the new stitches, I had to get, I received a call from Sgt. Banks. She let me know, the police were done collecting all the evidence they needed and have released the store back to me.

She, also, gave me a number to a company that specializes in cleaning up crime scenes. I called and made an appointment and they had an opening today at 2 PM.

I asked Jo to meet them because I wasn't ready to go back there yet. Now, I'm pulling up at Paul's office. Once I park, I lay my head back on the seat.

"We've been in a relationship," she corrects, "for over

three years. It started off as sex and an occasional dinner but after the first six months, things evolved."

"But you knew he was married?"

"I did but he said you all were just together for Kelsey. Look, I am not here to stake my claim on him because he's already mine but, like I said, I am tired of his lies."

"Let me guess, he said we were going to get a divorce?"

She nods, yes.

"And you believed him, even though he comes home to me, we take family vacations and pictures— "

"He also comes home to me; we take family vacation and pictures too. Lyn, I know this is a lot to take in, but Paul said, he's only staying because you're unstable."

I smirk, "and you're here now because you've realized what, he's been lying? Kandis, there is nothing unstable about me."

"No? Then why were you contemplating suicide, a few weeks back."

I look at her, anger beginning to build.

"I didn't come here to air your dirty laundry. I came to tell you to divorce him. You can keep your store, the house and your car because we don't want any of that. I only want him. Oh, and Kelsey, if she chooses to live with us."

"You've met my daughter?"

"Of course, I have. She's been a great big sister to our son."

"Wow, you all have a son?"

"Yes, he's two and a half and looks just like his father. Lyn, you can bounce back from this. Besides, I like you. You're a little on the heavier side but that was Paul's preference and you have friends who will support you through the divorce. Just don't make it hard because I fight for what I want."

I laugh. "So, do I but what I will not fight for, is a man who isn't worthy of it."

"Oh, he's worth it," she smirks.

A car door slamming pulls me out of my thoughts. I turn off the truck and get out.

Once inside, I go straight to Paul's office.

"Lyn, where have you been?" he asks when I walk in.

"That doesn't matter. I came to talk to you."

"Is everything okay? You look like you haven't slept in days. I'm worried about you."

"Don't be. I only came to tell you that I'm moving out."

"What? Wait," he says getting up to close the door. "What do you mean?"

"Well, I guess I need to rephrase that. I've moved out seeing I haven't been back to your house," I laugh.

"Baby, please don't do this. You've been through a lot; these last few weeks and now is not the time for you to be making drastic decisions like this."

"Drastic decisions?" I repeat. "A drastic decision is when you decide to play house with another woman, make a baby with her while you have a whole wife and daughter at home. Drastic is allowing the mistress to tell your wife because you didn't' have the balls. Drastic—"

"Lyn, I'm sorry."

"So, I've heard but what are you, exactly, sorry for Paul?" I ask, picking up the family picture of us, he has on his desk. "Are you sorry your baby momma showed up at my job, are you sorry you put our child in the middle of your affair or are you sorry you got caught?"

"I'm sorry for everything."

I throw the picture. "So am I. But the thing that irks me the most is, why couldn't you be honest with me? That day, I sat in the floor of our room and poured my heart out and I thought you were doing the same. You were the one who said we'd start over, after forgiving each other for our wrongdoing.

But noooo," I drag out. "Instead, you went back to your girlfriend and told her everything. You made me out to be some weak ass woman who couldn't control her home or her emotions."

"That's not true."

"Yes, it is. This woman knows everything about me but what's sadder, she knows everything about you. She gave you a child, she made you a home and—"

"It was a mistake. The only home I have is with you and Kelsey."

I chuckle. "You've lived this lie, for over three years. Baby, that's not a mistake, that's a common law marriage. What am I supposed to do with that? Should Kandis and I meet and agree to be sister-wives? Or better yet, maybe we should become a throuple."

"A what?"

"A relationship with three people, where you get to have your wife and mistress."

"I don't want that."

"Hell, you could have fooled me. Isn't this what you've had, all this time?"

"Lyn, what can I do to make this right? I will apologize and beg, for however long it takes but please don't leave me," Paul says grabbing my hand.

I snatch away. "The thing is, I don't want you to

apologize or beg. I only want you to leave me alone because all of this is just too much."

"Can we take some time apart and work on our marriage?"

"Paul, there is no longer a marriage. The trust we had is gone and I don't see how it'll ever be repaired. Not after this. You and Kelsey would lie about going on daddy, daughter weekends when you were probably doing family vacations with Kandis. Tell me I'm wrong."

He doesn't say anything.

"My point exactly. Goodbye Paul."

"This is some bullshit!" he yells. "I was willing to forgive you, after you cheated. Yea, I've made mistakes but nothing that can't be worked out. Lyn, we've both done things wrong."

"You're right, Paul but the difference between you and I, you caught feelings and created an entire life with your side piece. Me, I admitted my faults and the entire time, I thought you were admitting yours; it was a bold face lie. You left me, the same night, a day, two days or whatever later and went to her.

I bet y'all had a good laugh at Lyn's expense, too. Afterwards, you probably played with your son, bathed and put him to bed while she cleaned the kitchen and then you put her to sleep. Her words not mine."

"Please don't give up on me."

"I didn't. You gave up on me, the moment you chose Kandis." I exhale. "Paul, I'm done. I only came to tell you to your face because that's what grownups do."

"What about Kelsey?"

"What about her?"

"Lyn, this is going to devastate her."

"Well, let Kandis console her."

"Baby please, don't do this. I love you and want you. Lyn, I need you." He grabs my face. "Please—"

Before he can finish, his door opens. "Paul, I—oh, I'm sorry."

I turn and come face to face with Kandis.

"She works here? Wow," I say pushing him away from me. "Doesn't the help know how to knock on closed doors?"

"I didn't know he had company," she says looking me up and down while walking over to his desk.

"Company?" I laugh before punching her, square in the face. "Bitch, you got away with disrespecting me once, but I got time today." I grab her by her blazer. "Don't you ever think, for one second, you're doing something grand by sleeping with and having a baby by a married man. You'll always be second because you're comfortable being there. But good luck to you."

"Lyn stop before you bust your stitches again."

I shove her away from me and turn, giving Paul the same blessing before he has a chance to react.

"It's apparently obvious that you're either slow or don't care. Standing in my face talking all this crap, knowing she's working in our company. You're a piece of work."

"I'm sorry," he says wiping his mouth with the back of his hand.

"This is the last time you will ever make me look like a fool. I'm done and if there was a way, I could remove the slightest residue of you, from my heart I would because you make me sick."

Cam

"Oh my God, you're awake," Chloe screams as she rushes into the room with Kerri. Soon after Ray comes in.

Seeing them makes me cry, harder as they all gather around the bed hugging and kissing me.

"I'm sorry you all had to see me like this," I say hoarsely.

"Girl stop apologizing! All we need for you to do, right now, is get well and get your ass out of this hospital," Kerri replies.

"Can somebody get me some more water?" I request.

Chloe brings the cup over to me and my face must have registered the shock because they all laugh. "Chloe," I whisper, laying my hand on her stomach and she covers it with her hand.

"Yea, about that," she laughs. "You're going to be an auntie, again."

"Well, I see everyone is here. How are you feeling?" Dr. Cleaves ask.

"Like I've been through hell."

"I don't know what hell feels like, but you are one blessed woman. Your vitals are looking good but there is something we need to discuss. Would you like your friends to step out?"

"No, what is it?"

"We've been monitoring your urine output, creatine levels as well as the swelling in your legs and you're currently experiencing acute kidney injury. The good thing about this is that it's treatable and you'll survive."

"Will she need dialysis?" Shelby inquires.

"We're going to monitor her tonight and if her urine output doesn't increase, yes, at least until her kidneys recover."

I let out a loud cry and Kerri comes over to me.

"I know this is a lot to take in, but we will get you back home to your family. We'll move you to a regular room and continue to monitor you," Dr. Cleaves tells me.

"How long will she be here?"

"That depends on her healing. Cam, you suffered a great deal of trauma and what you're facing now, is the aftermath. It will take some time to recover, fully and you'll have to be patient. In the meantime, I highly recommend talking to our staff psychiatrist."

"A psychiatrist? For what? I didn't try to commit suicide; it was an accident."

"I understand but you've been through a lot and with you still experiencing the effects of your injury, speaking to a therapist can greatly help you cope." Dr. Cleaves explains.

"Cam, you can do this and the faster you get it started, the faster you can go home to your family," Shelby encourages.

"Fine! I don't seem to have a choice anyway."

"A choice about what?" Thomas ask, coming in.

"Talking to a psychiatrist," I answer him.

"Mr. Shannon, as I told your wife, we are moving

her to a regular room but she's suffering from acute kidney injury and may need a couple rounds of dialysis. I suggested meeting with a staff psychiatrist to help her process everything," Dr. Cleaves states.

"I'm in agreement with that."

"But—"

"Camille, look at where you are. This is not up for debate. You either get help or what I said before, still stands. You cannot continue down this path. You almost died, for God sakes."

"Fine."

"I'll be back, in a little while." Dr. Cleaves leaves out.

"We're going to let you all have some time," Shelby says. "The girls and I will come back tomorrow to check on you."

"Wait, where's Lyn?"

"She'll be here. Now, get some rest."

They each give me a hug before leaving.

Thomas sits in the chair beside the bed.

"Thomas, I am so sorry. I never intended for things to go this far."

"Camille, you need help and no matter how many times you apologize, that fact still remains because it shouldn't have come to this. Seeing you with a tube down your throat and not knowing if you'd make it was the hardest thing I've experienced." He sighs.

"Did the kids see me like this?"

"No, and it was hard keeping them from you. I had to lie and tell them you couldn't have visitors." He tells me.

"Thank you."

"I didn't do it for you, but I did it for them. Man, I'm tired because I've hardly slept, since you've been here and now that you're awake, you're still fighting the issue of getting help. Camille, what is it going to take for you to know you have a problem?"

"I made a mistake, but I don't have a problem."

He throws his hands up and stands.

"You almost died from overdosing on cocaine and you still don't think you have a problem? You need dialysis, for God's sake. Come on Camille, you're smarter than this."

"I didn't know it was cocaine."

"That's even worse."

"Thomas, I made a dumb mistake but that doesn't mean I need a therapist. All I need is a little time to get over this."

"Wow," he says rubbing his hand over his face. "You act like everything you've been through, these last seven days, was something off your bucket list."

"I'm not. I'm sorry for everything."

"No matter how many times you apologize, your actions are what matters."

"I know that, and I'll show you, but I don't need help."

"The choice is yours, Camille, but I will not keep having this same argument with you. You either get help or we're done."

"Are you really going to kick me out, now? Thomas, I need you and our children."

"When you're released from the hospital, you can move into the guestroom."

"The guestroom? That's my house too."

"Not as long as you refuse help. At this point, the guestroom is all I have to offer. Take it or leave it."

"Fine," I say.

"I'm going to go and get the kids, from school. Maybe seeing them will convince you to get some help."

"Wait, do they know?"

"No, they, along with your co-workers, were told you had pneumonia;" he says standing up.

"Thank you."

"Again, this wasn't for you. I did it for our children, but you need to think about your life, Camille, because the next time we gather at your bedside, it could be to say goodbye, for good."

Chloe

I finally decide to meet Todd. It's been a few days but with everything going on, it couldn't be helped. I'm standing outside of the hotel room, he's staying at and although I'm having second thoughts, I knock.

It takes a few seconds, but he opens it.

"Hey," he says, stepping back to let me in. "Thank you for coming. Can I get you something to drink?"

"No, I'm good. What's up? I thought you would have been gone back to Gatlinburg by now." I question, not bothering to sit.

"I just got back this morning. Would you like to sit?"

"No thanks."

"Chloe, I'm sorry for the way I handled things. When you said you were pregnant, and the baby is mine, it was like I couldn't think anymore. I never expected this."

"Neither did I, Todd and I apologize for the way you found out. I had plans on telling you, but I hadn't figured it out yet. With that said, I'll never force you to do something you don't want to. When the baby is born, we can get a DNA test and if you choose to be a part, we'll work out some sort of visitation. Now, is that it?"

"No, because I need to apologize too. I was a jerk and my mom told me so. The thing is, I dated a woman, a few years ago who told me the same thing and after spending months, waiting and falling in love with a baby; it turned out not to be mine."

"I'm sorry you went through that but I'm not that woman."

"Not to be rude but I don't know you well enough to know if that's true."

I chuckle. "You're right but what would I gain by lying to you? I don't need you or your money to survive."

"Maybe that's true but if this baby is mine, then I need to know who I'm getting involved with."

"Wow, are you always this arrogant?"

"I'm not arrogant but I will not allow another woman to hurt or take advantage of me, again."

"Dude, I get that you've been hurt but I will not pay the cost for somebody else. This is your baby but whether you're around or not, he or she will still be fine. As for continually going back and forth with you, how about this, I'll text you after the birth. In the meantime, you might want to see a therapist to deal with your past hurt."

*****

I am jolted from my sleep by somebody touching my face.

I bolt up.

"Chris, what the hell are you doing and how did you get in my house?"

He holds up a key. "I took it from Lauren," he smirks.

I snatch it from him and pull the comforter up

over me.

"You need to get out of my house."

"Chloe, come on. I know we're divorced but I wanted to see you."

When he reaches to touch my face, I smack his hand away.

"What do you think you're doing?"

"Damn it, can't you take a hint?"

I slide out of the bed, on the opposite side, away from him and put my robe on.

"The only hint I'm taking is that you've lost your mind, especially if you think I'm about to sleep with you."

He follows me down the hall.

"Why are you being so extra? It's not like you've ever had a problem sleeping with me before. Look Chloe, this doesn't have to be complicated. It's just sex," he tells me rubbing between his legs.

I laugh. "Negro, you wouldn't even have sex, with me, when we were married and now, you show up with a hard penis and expect me to open my legs—"

"Or your mouth."

"Bitc—Chris, get the hell out of my house."

I walk over and turn the knob, pulling the door open but he grabs me, pushing me against the wall. He reaches for my robe and when he gets ready to untie it ...

"Chloe?"

I jump at the sound of Todd's voice.

"Um, am I interrupting something?"

"Yes, you are and why are you in my house?" Chris questions, never releasing the string to my robe.

"I'm here to see Chloe but I can come back."

"Nah, you can wait outside because I only need a few minutes with my wife," Chris says turning back to me.

He pulls the string on my robe and it opens, revealing my stomach. Chris' eyes get big.

"Hold up, you're pregnant?"

I quickly tie my robe. "Whatever I am, it's not

your concern because this baby isn't yours."

"The hell you say. How many months are you?"

"Chris, get out of my house. You know as well as I do, we haven't had sex in months so I'm however many months that is."

"Oh," he laughs. "This entire time you acted as if I did something drastic when I broke our vows, but it looks like you broke them too."

"Whatever Chris. Our marriage is over, so it doesn't matter anymore. You are no longer my problem and I'm not yours. As for this baby, it isn't yours, thank God."

He walks up to me. "I can feed it until it looks like me though. Why don't you send your company away and let me show you?"

"Nah, I don't think that's an option," Todd says.

"Oh yea, says who?"

"The father of that baby," Todd says with his chest stuck out.

Chris laughs. "Aw, it looks like you found you a pretty boy. Well, I hope he's better at dealing with you than I was."

"Dude, if anybody dealt with anything, it was me who put up with your broke and pathetic tail, for far too long. Thank God, I came to my senses before we made anything together, especially a baby. Now, get out of my house and do not come back. If you do, I'll call the police."

"I'll be back after pretty boy Floyd is done with you," he says before I slam the door in his face. I turn back to Todd. "Look, I am not in the mood for anymore foolishness so, if you came here with something stupid in mind, show yourself out."

I walk into the bedroom when I hear my phone ringing.

"Are you and your husband getting back together?"

I silence my phone, sigh and look at Todd. "Hell no. Did that look like a happy reunion to you?"

"I was just asking."

"Well let me ask you something. What are you

doing at my house and how did you get my address?"

"I called your office and you weren't in. Since I still had your address, from when you gave it to me in Gatlinburg, I came here. I hope you don't mind."

"I sure do. I mind a whole lot because you have no right to show up here, unannounced."

"Chloe, I am not here to argue with you. I only came because I needed to apologize."

"Nawl, I've seen this movie and knows how it ends, I'm good. What? Did it feel good to be all macho, back there with your chest stuck out? Well, I don't need you coming to my rescue."

"I apologize if that's what you think I was doing. I only wanted him to take his hands off you."

"Whatever Todd, what do you want?"

"You were right when you said, I have no right projecting my insecurities on you. My last relationship left me scarred and although we don't really know each other, I want to believe you when you say this baby is mine."

My phone dings with a text notification. I turn to get it, but he grabs my arm.

"Chloe, I'm sorry. I've been a real jerk and you didn't deserve that. I know we don't know each other but I'd like to start over."

"Todd, please let my arm go."

"I apologize for grabbing you, but I need you to know that I am not some arrogant guy who treats women like this. If my mom and sister knew the things I've said, they'd beat me," he laughs. "It's just, when you told me you were pregnant, I was shocked. When I asked you to meet me at the hotel, it didn't go as I'd planned because I let doubt speak for me."

"Noted. Is there anything else because I need to take a shower and get dressed?"

"After you left the hotel, I couldn't stop thinking about you and the way I left things. I acted like a jerk and I can admit my fault. As a man it is my duty to take care of you and this baby, if it is mine."

"Todd, I don't want you to be a father because it

is your duty. I want you to be a father because you desire to be. For the third or fourth but final time, I'll give you a paternity test and if after the paternity test, you want to be a part of this baby's life, then you make that decision."

"But Chloe, I want to be with you, too."

I laugh. "Are you drunk or is this screw with Chloe day?"

"No," he says as my phone dings again with a text from Taylor.

I turn back and gasp at the sight of Todd being on one knee.

"When I said I want to be with you, I mean it. Chloe, will you marry me?"

"I must be getting punked. Dude, a week ago you were calling me a whore, then you've insinuated that I'm good at lying and now you've had a change of heart and want to commit your life to me?"

"Yes. Will you at least think about it?"

"Sure," I pause. "I thought about it and no Todd, I will not marry you. The next time I commit myself to a man, it's going to be the last time. I spent the last three years of my life with a man who didn't love me, and I will not make that mistake again. What I will do, is be open to raising this baby with you but for now, get up and show yourself out."

Shelby

Sunday morning and Brian and I are headed to worship. It feels good to be going, as a family because it's been a long time. We used to be members of a church, a while back but then we slacked off.

I'd sent all the girls a text, on yesterday, inviting them but none of them replied. I can't worry about them because I'm hoping today, is the day God moves us to join, here at High Point. We take our seats just as the Praise and Worship leader begins to sing, Break every Chain by Tasha Cobbs.

There is power in the name of Jesus. There is power in the name of Jesus. There is power in the name of Jesus, to break every chain, break every chain, break every chain. To break every chain, break every chain, break every chain.

I'm on my feet, with my hands lifted as the reality of how much I've missed being in the fellowship of Christ, flows through me. I've been so caught up in everything else that I've missed out on talking to the one person who could do it all, Jesus.

"There is power in the name of Jesus," I sing along. "There is power in the name of Jesus, to break every chain."

I feel someone touch me and it's Kerri, Chloe, Ray and Lyn. They sit, on the row in front of us and all I can do is smile. Then my smile fades because inwardly, I'm berating myself. Why did it take tragedy, losing stuff and the potential to lose people; for us to come back to church?

By the time the song is over, my spirit is heavier than it was before.

"You okay?" Brian leans over and ask.

"Yes baby, I'm good."

After going through the program, Pastor Reeves stands at the podium.

"Good morning High Point," she exclaims. "I pray you all came in with a spirit of due. Due, d-u-e, as in expected at or planned for at a certain time or my favorite definition, a person's right or what is owed to someone.

If you'll look at the screens, you'll see the scripture, Galatians 6:9, "*And let us not be weary in well doing: for in due season we shall reap, if we faint not.* I know it's customary for me to have you all stand but today, I want each of you to jot down this scripture.

Whether you put it in your notepad or your phone, make note of it. See, we're about a month from Thanksgiving and while we ought to be preparing our celebratory festivities of thankfulness, some of us aren't. The reality of the time is, some of us are in a dark spot and we got every emotion running through us but thanksgiving.

Sure, we're thankful but in the forefront of our mind is worry. Worry about bills, sickness, children, spouses, choices made and quite possibly regret. Sure, we're thankful that God allowed us to get up, thankful that we're in our right mind, thankful we have control of ourselves and not the prison guard and thankful we can move and didn't need the help of a nurse; but there are some trials and tribulations that will not leave us alone.

And somewhere, in the midst of wanting to be thankful, some of us have found ourselves toiling with the cares of this old world. Leaving us questioning, why is all this hell happening to me. Why am I the one whose storm seem to never end? Why am I the one who has to go through a sickness that might be unto death?

Well beloved, I come to speak to those of you who are in a season of feeling defeated because there has been no return on your investment. I'm talking to those of you who keeps checking the harvest and it still isn't ripe. Those of you who are feeling like it's time to throw in the towel, close the business, tear up the vision, file the divorce, destroy the plans or shut up the blinds and die.

God told me to tell you, in due season.

I know this might be hard to hear but truth is, not ever season of our life will be a season to reap. There are seasons, we have to go through spiritually, the same as what we go through naturally. Sometimes our season can be to plant and other times, we have to survive on what has been stored in the barnyard."

Lyn gets up and it looks like she's crying. I wave to the others to let them know I'll check on her. Making it to the door, I can see the tears falling so I grab her hand and take her into the bathroom.

"Lyn, talk to me. What's wrong?"

"Paul's baby's mother is here, and that little boy looks just like him. Shelby, why would he do this to me? After all this time, why couldn't he have been honest?" she sobs. "Do you know, he has the audacity to have her working in our business?"

"Lyn, I don't know why Paul chose to do this, but this isn't your fault. What this is, is your season to suffer but it won't last always. All you have to do is prepare, wait and then recover."

"But this shit hurts."

I look around to see if anyone else is in the bathroom because I didn't want them offended by her language.

"It hurts, Shelby."

"I know but it'll have to end."

"When though? Huh? When?" she hits one of the stall doors. "Shelby, I know I've messed up, in this life but this, all of this, is too much. It feels hard to breathe, sometimes."

"I know but Lyn, we've had a long while of getting the good of God and we didn't give up. We can't give up now, that we have to experience a storm."

"I hear you, but I need to get out of here. I don't even know why I came."

"Lyn, wait," I grab her arm. "Don't leave like this. Stay and we can have prayer with Pastor Reeves, again."

"No, I can't but tell the girls, I'll talk to them later."

I make it back into the sanctuary and Pastor Reeves is still preaching. As she closes her message and opens the doors of the church, I'm too far removed to even know if this was the Sunday to join.

As soon as church is over, the girls want to know what's wrong with Lyn, so I give them a quick rundown of the situation.

When we get to the door, Pastor Reeves and another lady is standing there, greeting the people.

"Wait," Chloe says, pulling us towards her.

"What's wrong?" we ask, looking at her.

"That's Todd's mother," she whispers and points.

"Who?" I ask.

"The lady standing there with Pastor Reeves."

"Okay? And? Go say hi so we can eat," Ray says pushing her towards them.

"No, I'm not doing that. What if she thinks I'm a floosy or something?"

"A what?" we laugh.

"Y'all know what I mean. Forget y'all."

"Girl, come on."

"Hey, it's Shelby, right?" Pastor Reeves asks.

"Yes ma'am, and this is my husband Brian, my

daughter Brinae and you may remember my sisters; that's Raylan, Chloe and Kerri. This is Kerri's son, MJ."

"I remember you," Todd's mother, Denise says to Chloe. "You're the young lady who's carrying my granddaughter."

"Todd told you?" Chloe questions with a look of shock and uncertainty.

"Of course," she beams, "do you know how long I've waited for this? Here's my card, you need to call me."

"Uh, yes ma'am."

Pastor Reeves laughs when Denise walks off. "You've all she's been talking about."

"Really, I, uh, I was expecting her to hate me," Chloe stammers.

"Girl, we all make mistakes. The blessing though, is learning from them. Anyway, how are the other young ladies?"

"Camille is doing better. She's in a regular room

now and will probably be discharged soon. As for Lyn, she was here but she had to leave."

"We'll continue to pray for them. It was good having you all visit us, again. Maybe soon, you'll find that you love it here and will join."

"Pastor Reeves, is it okay if I call your office to schedule some time, with you, for my husband and me? He was recently diagnosed with cancer and—"

"No need to go into detail. Call the office and my assistant will put you on the calendar."

Chapter 7

Lyn

By the time I made it to my car, I could barely see through the tears. Tears of fury and frustration that is causing me to hit the steering wheel and scream. Then my tears turned into uncontrollable sobs. I laid my head back on my seat and I cried.

The noise of people talking causes me to jump up. I realize church is ending. I start my car and drive off before the girls see me. I end up at the hospital, to visit Cam. I haven't seen her since she's woken up.

She's asleep, so I sit next to the bed and grab her hand. I sigh.

She turns.

"Lyn," she says as tears fill her eyes. "I've been worried about you. What happened to your neck?"

"It's nothing, we can talk about that later. How are you?"

"Other than having to do a few dialysis treatments, I'm okay. What about you?"

"I don't know."

"What's wrong? Talk to me."

"Paul has another baby, a son," I tell her as a tear fall. "I went to church, this morning, with Shelby and she was there. Cam, he's been cheating for three years and seeing this little boy felt like a kick in the gut. He's the splitting image of Paul.

You want to know what hurts the most? I asked him about having another baby, three to four years ago and he shot the idea down. He made me feel foolish for asking but he had a son, with her."

"Sister, this isn't your fault. Paul is a dumbass, but you cannot take the blame."

"I know but I feel like the biggest fool, Cam but not anymore. This was his last time hurting me."

"What do you mean? You didn't kill him, did you?"

"I want too but instead, I moved out. I haven't told the other girls, yet so please keep it between us."

"Where are you staying?"

"An apartment, downtown. It's one with security, in the lobby and everything. I can't wait for you to see it."

"Hell, maybe we can be roommates," she laughs. "Thomas is still pissed at me, but he offered to let me move back, in the guestroom."

"What do you mean, move back?"

"He put me out. The night everything happened, he'd packed my bags. That's how I ended up at the motel, but it was my fault. He gave me the choice of getting help or getting out—"

"And you chose the latter?"

"What else was I supposed to do? I don't need help," she says.

"Camille, sweetie, I'm sorry to break this to you but we all need help."

"Maybe you're right," she laughs, "but don't tell Thomas."

I lay my head on her hand.

"We've got to survive this," I tell her.

"Girl, we will be okay. We're the six pack and if

anybody can make it through trials and tribulations, it's us. We've seen death, sickness and all kinds of crap. This ain't nothing."

A nurse comes in.

"Mrs. Shannon, it's time for your dialysis."

"I'm going to go but I'll be back."

"Hopefully, I'll be able to get out of here tomorrow."

"Okay, well text or call if you need anything." I give her a kiss on the forehead. "I love you and I'm so happy you're okay."

"You're going to be okay too."

Walking to my car, I keep looking around because it feels like I'm being followed. I hear a woman scream and I jerk my head.

"Ah," I say when I move too fast and it hurts my neck.

I pick up my pace.

Damn, for a big bitch, you sure move fast.

I turn around, clutching my purse to me and when I turn back, a car horn blow.

"Ma'am are you okay?" a lady question.

"I'm okay."

I get to my car and hurriedly get inside, locking the doors.

"Get it together Lyn."

As I start my car, my cell phone rings with Paul's ringtone. I contemplated not answering, but I do.

"Yea."

"Lyn, where are you?"

"Why, Paul? What's up?"

"Can you please come by the house because Kelsey is crying herself sick about you moving out."

"No, I—"

"Please Lyn."

I hang up, without responding and thirty minutes later, I'm parked on the side of the street. I walk up to the front door and ring the doorbell.

Paul opens the door. "Why are you ringing the doorbell? This is still your house."

"No, it's not." I move pass him. "I'm here so what's up."

"Can you please drop the attitude? Your daughter needs you."

"Oh, now she needs me but for the last three years, she's had Kandis and her brother."

"His name is Paul, Jr."

"I really don't care. Why am I here?"

I walk into the living room to see Kelsey on the couch with her headphones in.

"What's going on?" I look back at Paul.

"Mom," Kelsey says sitting up. "You're here."

"Only because your dad said you were crying yourself sick."

"I lied," he says, "but it was the only way to get you to come."

"Damn, you're getting good at this lying thing. Goodbye Paul."

"Lyn, stop," he yells. "Stop running away and talk to us. Yes, I screwed up and I get you turning your back on me but not Kelsey. She's your only daughter."

"Is that supposed to make me feel better because in actuality, it makes me feel worse? Yes, Paul, she is my only daughter, yet she chose to keep your secret."

"You are right mom, I did. I messed up and I should have told you, but I didn't. What am I supposed to do now because I've tried apologizing, you will not accept it? I call you, but you won't accept those either."

"I don't want you to do anything, smart mouth assed girl. I don't know why y'all seem to think apologizing will make this better. It's not like you broke my favorite necklace or forgot my birthday. This was an affair. A WHOLE FREAKING THREE YEAR AFFAIR that both of you knew about."

"I couldn't tell you because it would break your heart," she says starting to cry.

"Please don't start the tears because I am no longer moved by those. Kelsey, your dad and I have been together since we were seventeen. We had you, when I was nineteen and it was a struggle. On days we felt like giving up, I had you to gain strength from.

When you were about three, we were facing another eviction, from yet another apartment and that night, you came and wrapped your arms around me and said, mommy, you'll always have me and daddy. From that moment on, I knew I'd always fight for y'all. I just never knew, y'all would one day stop fighting for me."

"We didn't."

"YES, YOU DID! Got damn it," I yell.

"Can we please just talk about this?" Paul pleads.

"Talk? What should we talk about? How you both betrayed my trust or maybe you want to know how it feels like my heart is being ripped out? I've been trying to understand what I could have possibly done to deserve this. Was I not good enough? Did I not pay enough attention? Was my cooking or house cleaning, that bad? What? Please tell me because everything I've done has been for my family."

Neither of them says anything.

"Say something," I demand.

"You didn't do anything, mom but I don't know what else to say. I can give you excuses or come up with something, but truth is, I was selfish and chose daddy's secret over you. But," she pauses, "I didn't think y'all were happy anyway. You didn't seem to mind all the times he would spend with her so, over time, I just didn't say anything. I'm sorry."

She gets her phone and headphones and turns to me. "I hope one day you'll forgive me," she says before walking over and kissing me on the cheek.

"Lyn, I should have been honest with you." Paul says. "I got so wrapped up and comfortable that—"

"Paul, I don't want to hear anymore. I'm done having this conversation because it doesn't change anything. Let's just agree that our time together is over."

"Do you really feel that way?"

"Uh, don't you? Maybe Kelsey is right about us not being happy. I mean, you've been living this double life, for three years and I never noticed. I only wish, you'd told me, you wanted out, instead of giving your baby's mother, the power to decide and then tell me. On top of that, she's working in a company that our blood, sweat, tears, hardships, declines, evictions and everything else paid for. Talk about a slap in the face."

"What else was I supposed to do? She needed a job to support our son."

"Wow," I smirk. "It's still about them. Do you not see how your choices are YOUR choices and has nothing to do with me, YOUR WIFE? You stand here, talking about wanting me back but your mistress is working in a business with our name on the door. You stand here, apologizing but if she were to call, right now, you'd drop everything."

"Lyn," he blows out a breath. "I don't know what to do."

"I do, let me go."

"Lyn, please," he begs, grabbing my arm. "I can't

let you go. You're all I know. You're my wife."

"Oh, I get it," I laugh. "She isn't what you thought she'd be, is she? She was good as the part time, baby momma, side chick but as the girlfriend, she sucks."

"She's not you," he says softly.

"But she's who you chose, sweetie and now, because she isn't fulfilling everything, as full time, you want me back? Nah, I'm good."

"Lyn, I'm here and I need you. Can't that be enough?"

"You can't be serious? You know what? I don't know who's more foolish, you for the shit you're saying or me for listening. Goodbye Paul and I mean it, for real."

Kerri

I'm sitting outside on the patio, with a cup of coffee and the monitor from MJ's room. Michael left, almost two weeks ago, for rehab and ever since, I've been thinking about our marriage.

My phone dings with a notification from this Bible Gateway App, I downloaded. I click on it to open the full verse.

"Therefore, since we have been justified by faith, we have peace with God through our Lord Jesus Christ. Through him we have also obtained access by faith into this grace in which we stand, and we rejoice in hope of the glory of God.

Not only that, but we rejoice in our sufferings, knowing that suffering produces endurance, and endurance produces character, and character produces hope, and hope does not put us to shame, because God's love has been poured into our hearts through the Holy Spirit who has been given to us," I read out loud. "Romans five, verses one through five. I need to send this to the girls."

I get ready to open my messages, but I get another notification from my email. I open and see it's from Michael.

Kerri,

As I laid in the bed, across from the room I've shared with you, these past eleven years, I couldn't help but cry. I was praying, you didn't hear me because I wouldn't have been able to get out what I needed to say, then.

However, while I was sitting in the airport, preparing to board the plane that would take me to Jackson, MS; to a rehab, God gave me the strength to write this. I know you're wondering why you're getting this now, but I delayed the delivery. I wanted to give you a chance to think about what I asked for. Forgiveness.

Kerri, I love you.

Man, I've loved you with every part of my heart since the day I met you, at that bus stop. You were carrying a box of cupcakes, you'd baked, for your friend's birthday and they smelled so good. You must have heard my stomach growling because you offered me one. LOL.

Kerri, I'm sorry.

I'm so sorry for abandoning you. I made myself a vow, before I even met you, that I'd never abandon someone I love, like my mom did to me but I did. Although I know how badly, being abandoned feels, I still did it to you and our son.

I tried to fight it but there were these voices, in my head that kept telling me I needed to leave you before you left me. I know you've never given me a reason to believe you would, but the enemy played a sick game, by using my past against me and I lost.

Kerri, my mom walked out on us, when I was fourteen. She told my dad she had a business meeting, out of town but she never came back. Turns out, she was in a relationship with the woman, she was starting a business with, and that woman didn't want children. My mom chose her and her business over us.

After she left, my dad turned into this cold, angry shell

of a person. Every word out of his mouth, was against women. He'd planted seeds of doubt, early on and I didn't know how deep they were until you started to open your business. Instead of being truthful with you, I turned to alcohol because it's what my dad turned too.

I see now that this is a generational curse that I have to break before I pass it to MJ. Anyway, they're calling my flight. You don't have to respond to this, but I wanted you to know how I felt and to ask you, again, to forgive me.

I love you Kerri Davis and I hope we can rebuild from this with no more secrets. Kiss MJ for me.

Michael.

I wipe the tears that were falling before hitting reply.

Michael,

I don't know when you'll get my reply but thank you. Thank you for your honesty but more importantly, thank you for being willing to get help. I've been praying for God to show me a sign, as it relates to our marriage and I don't know if this is it, but we'll see. I love you too and I look forward to seeing the new man that will emerge from this.

Kerri.

I lay the phone down before closing my eyes.

"Dear God, I know I haven't always served you, fully but forgive me. I've taken your grace for granted and used your favor, foolishly yet you've kept me. You kept me, long after you should have given up on me and for that I'm grateful. Thank you, God, for even giving me another chance to tell you thank you.

Now, as I sit here, all I ask is for you to guide me. I've been too long, out of your will and I can't do it any longer. God, I need you to tell me, what you'd have me to do concerning my life, my friendships and my marriage.

Then, give me the strength and wisdom to be obedient to what you say. God, I may not have always acted like it, but I trust you. I may not have always shown it, but I trust you and now, I need you to move. In your name, I pray. Amen."

Shelby

"Hey, calm down," I tell Brian.

"I'm just ready to get this over with. It's already bad enough, they've pushed the appointment out."

"I know but stop all the shaking." I put my hand on his leg.

"James," the nurse calls after about ten minutes.

"Right here," Brian says, getting up and grabbing my hand.

When we get back to the doctor's office, I can see the look of worry on his face. Hell, I'm also worried and my heart is racing but I can't let him see it. The last thing we need is the both of us being nervous.

I've been reading on Brian's condition and it left me with more questions. I pull out my notepad just as the doctor walks in.

"Good Morning."

"Good morning Dr. Harper, this this is my wife,

Shelby."

"It's nice to meet you Shelby. I can see from your notepad that you've come prepared," he smiles before sitting behind his desk. "That's a good thing. Now Brian, I don't know how much your other doctor told you, so I'll start from the beginning. First thing, I know being here is nerve wrecking and it doesn't help that we've put this off but relax."

Brian looks at me and I smile.

"Brian, I know, from your chart, the previous doctor thought you have what's called glioblastoma. However, I've since got some additional scans from radiology and what you have is cerebral convexity meningioma. This form is a slow growing tumor that grows from the protective membranes that cover the brain and spin.

I'm writing and trying to follow what the doctor is saying.

"Shelby," he says to get my attention. "I know this is a lot, but I'll give you information on it. Listen, Brian, this tumor is a grade two. This means it's a bit more aggressive and has a higher risk of reoccurrence, but it can be treated.

Most times there are no symptoms, as this tumor can grow for years. Although it's crazy to say, thank God for your headaches and you getting them checked."

"What do you recommend as far as treatment options?" Brian questions.

"Usually, with this type of tumor, we watch and wait. With you, I'm going to try some medicinal therapy to shrink the tumor. If your headaches start to get worse, then I'll perform surgery. The procedure is called a craniotomy."

"Then he'll be cured?" I ask.

"I wish I could tell you yes but right now, I don't know. During the surgery, samples of the tumor will be taken to confirm the grade and type. I'm also hoping, I can get the entire tumor during surgery."

"If you don't?" Brian questions.

"Then you'll need radiation. I will not lie to either

of you, this will not be easy but it's treatable. There's always a downside to surgery but I'm a man of faith and I believe God allows what He has already ordained. Brian, you're young and otherwise healthy, which helps. I know this is a lot of information and I'm sorry you're both having to deal with this, but we'll get through it."

Brian grabs my hand.

"Are you experiencing any other symptoms other than headaches?"

"No."

"Have you had any trouble with your balance?"

"A little."

"I'm going to schedule for you to have some tests run, this afternoon. Once I have the results back, we'll discuss surgery. In the meantime, I'll give you a prescription. Get it filled and start it, as soon as possible. I don't want to take the chance on your symptoms progressing to seizures."

"Whatever you think, Dr. Harper, I'm willing to try."

"Stop by Rita's desk and she'll give you all the information you need."

Brian was very quiet on the ride home from the hospital, after having the tests done.

"What are you thinking?" I ask him.

"I'm just trying to process everything. Shelby, what if—"

"No Brian, there is no what if. You're going to be fine because God wouldn't take you from me. Not now."

"We have to be realistic, Shelby."

"I understand but right now, I have to believe you'll survive this, and we'll be on a beach somewhere, soon."

*****

A few days later, Brian and I walk into High Point.

"Pastor Reeves, thank you so much for seeing us."

"Of course," she says giving Brian and I a hug.

"Come on in. Can I get either of you something to drink?"

"We both decline.

"I see that you all are needing prayer. You don't have to go into much detail, but I'd like to know a little, just to be sure we're all praying for the same thing."

I look over at Brian whose leg is shaking.

"Brian has been diagnosed with cancer, of the brain. His doctor says it's treatable but it's a dangerous surgery. We don't know what to expect but we know, we can't do this without God. Pastor Reeves, we used to be devoted to a church but then, we slacked off. Until we started visiting here, we hadn't been to church in years."

"Shelby, God doesn't shun or forget you because you haven't been to church, in a while. Yes, the bible says, do not forsake the assembling of ourselves together but it's what you do, outside these four walls that truly matter. Brian, is there anything you want to add?"

He opens his mouth but the only sound that comes out is a cry.

"I'm sorry," he says.

"No need to apologize. Let's pray."

She and I stand and she lays her hand on Brian's shoulder.

"Dear God, it is your servant, petitioning your throne. God, I ask you to give me power to speak, in this moment. Use me, oh God, converting my mouth into your mouthpiece and my hands into your vessels of healing. Increase in me, that my prayer reaches your ears, for your son, who is sitting before me, in need of you.

God, we know what the doctor said, and we know what the tests show but we still trust you. Even when we don't understand, we'll wait until you move because we know; you don't fail. God, tonight, have your way. You have the power to shrink tumors, stop pain, remove cancer and stay the hand of death. God, we know this because we've seen you work in others.

Now, if you'd be so kind, do it again. You healed a woman who was bleeding for twelve, long years. You healed a man, laying by the pool of Bethesda, sick from birth. You've healed men of leprosy and blindness. All I ask, of you, tonight, do it again. You've healed cancer before, do it again. You've strengthened and restored before, do it again. You've come to our rescue before, do it again.

God, we trust your plan and however you decide to turn this thing, father, do it. We don't know the plan you have for Brian, but we trust you. Whether, you heal on this side or your side, we'll still call you wonderful. Whether healing is on this side or your side, we'll still call you healer. Whatever your will is, we'll still call you way maker.

God, we trust your plan, concerning us because we know that if we trust you, you'll give us the strength to endure whatever we have to face. Thank you, Father. Thank you for what you're doing or will do. Thank you for already making provisions, we don't even see. Thank you for already providing the things, we don't even know we need.

And tonight, before we say amen, release peace over this family. Surround them with the courage and strength to press on. Allow them to see you, in every part of their life, knowing you'd never leave or forsake them. God, we thank you, in advance for things our eyes haven't seen, nor ears heard. By your might, God, we do pray. Amen."

"Amen."

"Thank you, Jesus," Brian exclaims. "Thank you, God."

He bends over and Pastor Reeves, grabs the oil from her desk and put some in her hand, before touching Brian's head. When she closes her eyes, she begins to speak in tongue.

After some time, she lays her hand on my forehead. When she's done, she pulls me into a hug.

"Pastor Reeves," Brian says, "I don't know how to thank you."

"You don't owe me a thanks because I'm only

doing what Jesus would. Anytime you need me, call me."

"Can we call you Pastor because I'd like for us to become members of High Point?" Brian asks, standing up.

Inwardly, I am screaming with joy and outwardly, my tears are falling. Pastor Reeves looks over at me. I smile and nod, wiping my face.

"Of course, you can. Have both of you been baptized?"

"We have."

"Do you both believe God sent His only Son, Jesus, to give us right to repent of our sins?"

"We do."

"And you both want to become members of High Point Christian Church?"

"We do."

"Then I extend my hand to each of you, giving you all rights and privileges as any other member. Welcome home."

Cam

"How are things, since you've been home? I know when we spoke, in the hospital, you told me that your relationship with your husband was up in the air. Is that still the case?"

"Yea but he'll come around. I'm giving him space to deal with things, his way."

"And what way is that?"

"Giving him space," I say, again, matter-of-factly. "He seems to think I need help, so here I am."

"You don't think you do?"

"No but don't get me wrong, I'm here because I want to be. Nobody is forcing me."

"Hmm," he says writing. "Have you had a craving for any drugs?"

"No and I wish people would stop asking me that. I made a mistake but I'm not a drug addict. I get that my family and friends are worried about me and I'm sorry for putting them through that but I'm not an addict."

"Then why did you turn to drugs?"

I shrug.

"Use your words Cam. You're a grown woman who made a choice to use drugs, twice that we know of. I'm pretty sure you know why?"

"Because I could. Is that a good enough answer?"

"If that's your truth."

"It is. I used drugs because I could and just like everything else, I thought I'd get away with it, but it didn't turn out like I'd thought. Oh well."

"Are you always this self-righteous?"

"I'm confident, Dr. Nelson."

"No, you're delusional if you think you don't have a problem. Cam, you overdosed on a cocktail of cocaine and whatever else. You were in the ICU for days while your family prayed, you'd survive."

"I did."

"No, you're alive but this isn't surviving. All you did was get well enough to go right back to your drug or drugs of choice. What's going to happen the next time, you do *something like this?"*

"I'll plan better," I smile.

"Why are you here?"

"Because my insurance pays for it."

I snap out of my thoughts of therapy with Dr. Nelson. He's a cool therapist, but I don't need him because I'm good. Anyway, it's been almost two months, since I woke up in the hospital, scared out of my mind. Dr. Cleaves and his staff ran some additional tests and thank God, after a few rounds of dialysis, my kidneys are now functioning properly.

I have to be tested, regularly in order to ensure there are no more residual effects of the drugs but other than that, Dr. Cleaves said I'm blessed.

Yes, I'm back home but still sleeping in the guestroom until Thomas believes, I've changed. I roll my eyes at the thought as I sit on the side of the bed, reflecting on something the therapist said I needed to do.

Well, I'm not really reflecting but I have to make

Thomas think I'm taking this seriously. Hell, the stuff they ask you in therapy is ridiculous and for people who really need it. Not Cam.

Dr. Nelson wants me to journal some of things that were going through my head, before the overdose. Truth is, the only thing that keeps coming up is, how stupid I was to use so much, at one time. But I can't write that, now can I?

I let out a long sigh as I look over this piece of paper that's been starring back at me for over an hour. Some twelve-step stuff, blah blah.

"Camille," I jump at the sound of Thomas' voice. "Are you okay?"

"Yea, just going over some stuff that Dr. Nelson gave me," I reply, holding up the journal.

"What is it?"

"Reflecting on the things that drove me to the point of using drugs. I just don't know what came over me. This person, the old person before this, it's not who I am. And I'm sorry for hurting you and our children."

"I'm glad to hear therapy is working and that you're sticking with it."

I smile and nod.

"To be honest, I didn't think you were serious about therapy."

"Thomas, it's been two months and I've showed you that I'm changing. What more do you want?"

"We'll see."

"Can't you give me a little credit?" I ask getting angry.

"I will when you show me, you're worthy of it."

I roll my eyes and throw the middle finger to his back before I finish getting dressed for our girl's night at Chloe's.

An hour later, I'm backing out of the driveway, when my phone rings. I press the Bluetooth button on the steering wheel.

"This is Camille."

"Mrs. Shannon, hey, I hope I didn't catch you at a bad time.

"No, Mr. Prosecutor, what can I do for you?"

"I was hoping you had a few minutes to talk about a case."

"Um," I say looking at the time. "Is this a case or a case, case."

"A case, case."

"I'm actually headed to meet my girls, but I have about 45 minutes to spare."

"Can I meet you, now?" he asks.

"Where?"

"What part of town are you headed?" he questions.

"East Memphis."

"Clarke Tower, on Poplar?"

I smile. "I'll see you in twenty."

I pull into the parking lot, looking around for his truck and when I didn't see it, I park and wait. After a few minutes, I see him pull in, next to me. I grab my keys and get out, getting into his truck.

"You're looking good," he smiles, "for a sick person."

"Thanks, but I'm not sick anymore. You know it'll take more than pneumonia, to keep me down." I smile knowing it was a bold face lie.

"When are you going back to work?"

"After the New Year. Why? Did you miss me kicking your ass in court?"

"Girl, please!" he laughs. "No, but I did miss that mouth."

"Oh, is that what you called me for. To see what this mouth can do?"

He reaches into the backseat and I take a moment to look at the print, between his legs. It's been a while since I've had some and I'm horny. Thomas is acting funny and—

He clears his throat and I laugh.

"You see something you want?" he questions.

"I do, actually but I shouldn't. I'm trying to do better, and I promised my therapist, I wouldn't indulge in any extracurricular activities."

"That's sweet," he says unfastening his pants and rubbing himself. "But I know the old Cam is in there and she wants to play because I can see it in your eyes. How long has it been?"

"You're so wrong?" I tell him, while watching him stroke himself.

"How long Cam?"

I look around.

"Too long," I yell, "but I can't risk getting caught."

"Nobody can see in," he assures.

I tap my hands on the door.

"If I get caught, I'm kicking your ass."

I reach over the console to touch him. He's so hard that my mouth is watering to taste him. I lean over, taking most of him inside and he moans, placing his hand on the back of my head.

His moans get louder and when I feel him tense up, I stop and climb over the console. Lifting my dress, I lower myself onto him.

Grabbing the back of the seat, I move slowly, at first before picking up the pace. I wait until my orgasm is done before, I move myself off of him, to help him finish. Covering him with my mouth again, I allow him to release himself into my mouth.

"Damn," he breathes.

I get settled into my seat and look over at him. His head is laid back and his eyes are closed. I take the water bottle, from his console and drink from it.

"Damn, you got me late. I'll see you when I return to the office."

I get out of his truck and walk back over to my car. I open the door and reach in, taking some wipes from my purse. I wipe between my legs and throw them under the car before getting in and driving off.

Chloe

"Hey," I say after opening my door to Todd, "what are you doing here?"

"I apologize for popping up, but I wanted to stop and check on you and the baby, and to see how your Thanksgiving was."

"My thanksgiving was great but you didn't think to call or text?"

"I didn't know if you'd answer because we haven't really spoken, over the last two months so—"

"So, you thought showing up would be the best thing? Look Todd, if you're coming to ask for my hand in marriage, don't. If you're here to question the paternity of this baby, don't." I say as the oven's timer goes off in the kitchen.

"What are you cooking? It smells good."

"Don't change the subject. Why are you here?"

"Chloe, I'm not here to argue. Every time we've

tried to have a conversation, it never goes well."

"And you thought, popping up would change that, this time?"

"No, but I hope it will. Can we talk, please?"

"Todd, tonight isn't good because we're having girl's night here and I'm trying to finish this pasta dish, take a shower and find something to squeeze in before they get here."

"What kind of pasta?"

I heavily sigh. "It's a basil pesto, tortellini with chicken and sausage."

"How about this? You go shower and change while I finish cooking and then we can talk until they arrive."

I look at him.

"I'm only trying to help. And you look good, by the way."

"Stop lying. My feet are swollen, I can only get my hair in a messy bun and my body has outgrown most of my clothes."

"You still look good, to me," he adds.

I wave him off and go into my bedroom. Thirty minutes later, I'm standing in front of my mirror, thinking back on the meeting I had with Todd's mom, a few weeks back.

"Mrs. French," I say walking up to her table.

"Chloe, please have a seat."

"Let me apologize for taking so long to call you but I didn't know what I'd say to you."

"Is this my son's baby?"

"Oh, okay, well let's get right to it."

"Chloe, you seem like a fine young lady, but my son has been down this road before."

"I'm aware, Mrs. French—"

"It's Ms. but call me Denise."

"Denise, Todd told me what happened to him, however I'm not in the business of lying to a man, especially about paternity of my child. As I've told Todd, I don't need him or his finances."

"I didn't mean to imply you were but he's my only son. I don't normally interfere in his business, but I've been

waiting for this day, for a while now and I just don't want to be disappointed again."

"I can assure you, Mrs. French, I am not trying to run game on your son. This is Todd's baby and I'll willingly give him a DNA test when he or she is born but I will not keep going back and forth. This is tiring, no offense."

"None taken but I hope you can understand where we're coming from. Chloe, I don't know what happened between you and Todd but if you can work it out, do so. Now, let's get you some food. I can't have my granddaughter starving."

"You really think it's a girl?"

"I know it is," she smiles.

"Chloe?"

"I'll be right there," I reply shaking off the thoughts.

I finish getting dressed in an oversize maxi, flats and brush my hair. Walking back into the kitchen, Todd is pulling bread from the oven. I look around and he's set up plates and everything.

"Wow. Was I gone that long?"

"No. You'd done all of the major stuff and I only had to finish the sauce and bread. I went ahead and got the plates down because I didn't want you reaching. I also made lemonade with what I found in the refrigerator. One is spiked, and one isn't."

"You didn't have to do all this but thank you because I'm tired," I cringe.

"You okay?"

"Yea, the baby has been extremely busy today," I reply sitting on one of the stools. He brings me a glass of lemonade. "Todd, why are you here and being so nice?"

"To make up for all the times I haven't been. Chloe, I've been a real ass to you and I'm sorry. If you'll let me, I want to start over by taking you out on a date."

"A date? Todd, I'm almost seven months pregnant."

"Which still gives us, at least, three months to

make things right. Will you please give me a chance to get to know you?" he pleads.

"How do you suppose we do that? You live in Gatlinburg, remember? Where you have an entire life and I don't want to set myself up for expectations of you that—"

"That I can't keep," he says, finishing my statement. "I won't lie and say this will be easy but I'm willing to try, if you are. Will I make some mistakes along the way? I'm sure but I won't ever make a promise I have no intentions of keeping.

I know we have a lot of things to learn about one another, things to hash out, but for the time being I am here. As for Gatlinburg, I've discussed things with my business partner and we've decided, he will take over the day to day operations there and I'll stay here."

"Just like that? You're going to uproot your life, for me, when a few months ago, you didn't believe a word coming out of mouth."

"Chloe, it's not that I didn't believe you but I've

been hurt. Furthermore, I've prayed about this and I know it's the right decision. As for moving back to Memphis, it was a part of my plan for opening the new restaurant. The baby just put things in motion quicker," he laughs. "I will have to go back to Gatlinburg at the end of the week to finalize a few things, but I plan to have everything done before the baby arrives. I know I've missed out on a lot, already and I don't plan on missing anything else."

"Well damn!"

"Did I say something wrong?"

"No, it seems you've figured everything out."

"I didn't mean to overstep. It's just, I like you and regardless of how things started with us, we're about to be parents, to a little girl, as per my mother."

I smile. "She is adamant about that, isn't she? I'm guessing, she told you about our meeting?"

"Yes, and I apologize because I had no idea, beforehand but please don't think I'm a momma's boy. She's never done that before."

"No need to apologize. She's only looking out for her son, which I can appreciate because I never had a mother who would, willingly, do that for me."

The doorbell rings.

"Shoot, that must be the girls."

"I'll get it, if you don't mind."

He gets ready to walk out but I cry out in pain.

Chapter 8

Lyn

"Prosecutors with the District Attorney's office has decided not to charge a woman in connection with the death of Xavier Toliver. If you may remember, Toliver was killed on September 24th, during, what officials have stated, the commission of rape. The prosecutors' office and investigators state, evidence collected shows the victim acted in self-defense when she stabbed Toliver. He died, at the scene, from his injuries. The woman's name has not been released."

I snap out of my thoughts, when my phone rings. I clear my throat and answer, putting it on speaker.

"Lyn, hey, are you okay?"

"Jo, I'm good. What's up?"

"Are you sure? You don't sound good."

"I'm fine, I'm actually about to meet the girls. How have things been at the store?"

"Everything is good. The painters finally finished

repainting the store and all the new inventory, you approved, has been ordered. The only thing left is the accounting."

"I've taken care of it, for this month but I'm thinking of getting someone to handle it, for a while so I can take some time off. In the meantime, thank you for handling the store. You have signing power to handle what needs to be done and once I get the accountant, squared away, I'll send you the information."

"No thanks needed. I'm here for you but are you sure, you're okay?"

"I'm fine, Jo, seriously. Just take care of my store, okay?"

"I will but if you need anything, call me."

I release the call and lock the phone, before laying it beside me. I look at the front of Chloe's house and contemplate not going in.

A knock on the window scares me.

"You aren't thinking about skipping out on us, are

you?" Ray asks.

I smile, turn the car off and open the door.

"I was, actually."

"Lyn, you don't have to stay all night, but we've missed you and we're worried about you."

I sigh. "Ray—"

"Please, for me," she says looking sad.

"Okay," I relent.

She smiles and grabs my arm as we walk up to the door and ring the bell.

"Todd?" Ray and I say, surprised. "What are you doing here?"

"Ladies, I'll explain later but something is wrong with Chloe."

We rush into the living room.

"Chloe, what's wrong?"

"It's nothing," she says. "Todd is overreacting."

"You were doubled over in pain."

"The baby is just moving, a lot."

"Are you sure? Let us call your doctor or take you to the ER, to be on the safe side."

"No, everything is fine," she says as the doorbell rings again. "Can y'all get that and let me talk to Todd? I'll meet you in the kitchen."

We go and open the door to Kerri and Shelby.

"Hey ladies," they both sing.

We exchange hugs before walking into the kitchen.

"Where's Chloe?"

"She's talking to Todd, in the living room."

"Todd's here?"

Ray shakes her head. "He said Chloe was having some pain, but she assures us, she's fine."

"Lyn, you okay? Lyn?"

"Huh, what did you say?" I ask when I realize she's talking to me.

"Are you okay? You seem to have zoned out."

"Did you all see on the news about the prosecutor not charging me?"

"Yeah, but we all knew this would be the outcome. Lyn, you had every right to defend yourself against a monster who raped you."

"I know," I cry, "but I still took a man's life.

"This isn't your fault." Shelby tells her, wrapping her arm around me.

"I just wonder, how would things have played out, had I not been so angry at Paul. This boy had been flirting with me, the entire time he delivered to the store, but I always turned him down."

"He was your delivery driver?" Kerri asks.

"Yeah and he made a few passes at me, but I'd always stop it because he was young but that day, I allowed him to come in and kiss me."

"Did you tell him no?" Shelby asks.

"Yes but—"

"There's no but. No means no and regardless of what Paul did and how upset you were, you said no."

"Who said no?" Cam questions, strolling in.

"Well, if you don't look all Cam like, with this damn dress on for girl's night." Ray laughs causing Cam to twirl.

"Now, who said no to something."

We all look at each other.

"What?" Cam questions.

"The night you overdosed, I was raped," I tell Cam.

I fill her in on all she missed while being in the hospital. Her mouth is open, and her eyes are full of tears.

"Cam, why are you crying?"

"Because I wasn't there. My selfishness caused me to be away from you all, when you needed me and I'm sorry."

"Girl, hush because you were in no shape to help us. Hell, we could barely help ourselves," Ray tells her.

"What else have I missed, since it's taken y'all two months to give me the tea?"

"Justin is gay, Chloe is divorced and pregnant by Todd, Mike is in rehab, Brian is sick, and Paul has a whole other family. Did I miss anything, ladies?" I question, looking at them.

"Now, what kind of flip, flopping, foolishness is going on here? Damn, I can't even overdose, without all hell breaking loose," she says. "I don't even know what to say."

"How do you think we feel?"

"I need a bottle of wine," I tell him.

"What did I miss?" Chloe asks, walking in.

"Really Chloe?" Kerri laughs.

Ray

"What? I was talking to Todd," she says with a smirk.

"Hmm, so what's going on with you and Chef French?" I inquire.

"Nothing, well, I don't know. He wants to get to know each other before the baby comes."

"That's what's up," Cam says, causing us to look at her. "What? I think it's cool that he's willing to get to know you, for you and not just his baby's mother. This is his baby, right? You wouldn't be lying to that man, would you?"

"Hell no. I probably would have lied to Chris' pitiful ass, because I can't see myself raising a Chia Pet with him, but not to Todd. This is his baby."

"Aite because I'll sign you up for Maury," Cam laughs.

"While you're all up in people's business, what's

up with you? We haven't had a chance to really get together and talk, since everything happened."

"Can we eat first?" Kerri asks.

We fix our plates and drinks before moving into the living room. We spend the next hour eating, drinking and laughing. After cleaning the kitchen, we go back and get settled.

I moved out," I blurt, and everybody stops.

"You what? To where and when?"

"I got an apartment, downtown about two and a half months ago."

"Lyn, you didn't have to do that because you could have moved in with us," Shelby says.

"I know but you and Brian have enough to deal with, without another houseguest and I need my own space. Since the attack and finding out about Paul, I need some time to think things over."

"You're talking about Paul having an outside baby?" Cam inquires.

"That and the fact, he's been living a lie for over three years and Kelsey knew."

"Kelsey knew her dad was cheating and didn't tell you? Oh, hell nawl," Cam says. "I'd beat Courtney's ass."

"That has definitely crossed my mind, believe me."

"How's your relationship with her, since everything?"

"There isn't one because I can't stop thinking of how they both betrayed me. The worse part, they think apologizing makes it all go away. Y'all I've been so angry that, right before I moved out, I tried to break every picture in our living room. The only thing that stopped me was, busting my stitches open."

"Lyn, I know how you feel because this mess with Justin has me the same way and my only saving grace, that stopped me from killing him, was my children."

"Maybe we should get Cam's therapist number," Kerri says. "It looks like we can all use the help."

Cam doesn't say anything.

"Camille, you are still getting help, right?" I ask.

"Define help," she retorts before sipping her wine.

"As in therapy, talking to someone and actually listening?"

"Yea, I've been a few times."

"But?"

"But, it's not for me. I don't like folk all up in my business," she says. "However, before y'all start, I am going because it gets Thomas off my back."

I touch her hand. "Cam, I love you sweetie, but we all know, this therapy won't do you any good unless you go for you."

"I don't need therapy. Therapy is for people with real problems."

"Real problems," Shelby repeats, "and yours aren't? Camille, you overdosed and was in the hospital for over a week. Not to mention the dialysis."

"Shelby, please don't start preaching," Cam tells her. "The night, I overdosed, Thomas and I had a huge fight and he put me out. He literally packed my bags and kicked me out. He was right to do it because I was spiraling, and I didn't realize how bad it was, but I didn't intentionally set out to overdose.

I thought I could control everything, like I've always done but I couldn't. And when I got home, he gave me an ultimatum to either get help or leave and being me, I said—"

"I don't need help," we all say.

"I don't," she replies rolling her eyes. "Yes, I messed up but when I left the house, that night but that's because I was angry and none of you would answer my calls. I don't blame y'all though because, after LA, I wouldn't have answered my calls, either. Anyway, I was pissed and in, f the world mode.

I stopped at a liquor store and drove until I ended up at a motel. There was a young lady there who came to my room, because I was screaming and talking to myself.

At first, I refused her but when she said she had something to make me forget my problems, I jumped at the chance. I had no idea what she gave me but after a minute, I guess I got what I'd been wishing for, to quiet the thoughts in my head."

"God has a way of getting our attention, doesn't He?" I ask.

"What do you mean?"

"Look at all we've endured; these last few months. Divorce, sickness, attacks; hell, you name it. Pastor Reeves said something, when she was at the hospital, that day. Hold on," I tell them grabbing my phone. "She said, God is allowing each of you to suffer differently yet at the same time. Please do not curse this test as it'll be what's needed to strengthen you and your faith."

"She ain't lying."

"I've been praying, a lot lately and I'm thankful to Shelby for talking us into going back to church with her. I don't know if she told y'all but me and my children, all joined, a few Sundays ago. It has been one of the best decisions because the children are able to focus on something more than Justin's infidelity and our divorce. A divorce, he's making hard."

"What are you going to do?"

"Keep fighting until he signs them papers. In the meantime, I've signed us up for some therapy because I know I can't fix this on my own." I take a breath. "Enough of that and to change the subject to more happier things, I was going through a box of old stuff, when I was packing Justin's crap. Guess what I found?"

"What?"

"Do y'all remember the time, after we'd been at TSU for a week and Cam got caught by campus police, having sex on the football field and we had to go and bail her out?"

"Hell yea," Lyn laughs. "She was sitting in jail in a mini skirt, handmade tube top and no panties. It was hilarious."

I reach into my pocket and pull out an old polaroid picture.

"Oh my God, Raylan Greer, no you didn't!" Cam

screams, snatching it from me.

"This wasn't my fault," she says handing the picture to Lyn. "I told, I think his name was James, not to let his pants drop. He did and when the cops showed up, he couldn't even get off me. I was so mad."

We all burst into laughter.

"Man, the memories I've made with all of you." Lyn says, her voice trailing off.

"Lyn, you okay?"

"I wish I could reclaim the time I lost," she tells us.

"Don't we all," Shelby says. "However, if there's anything I've learned these past months, it's to take nothing for granted and although we can't get the time back, we can take advantage of the time we have left."

"That's what I've been trying to tell y'all," Cam says. "Live life to the fullest, enjoying every moment."

"True but with wise decisions and prayer because we've seen what happens when we place God on the back burner. Not saying that we'll never suffer again but maybe, the next time storms come, we'll be more prepared." Shelby says.

"I agree because this attack, almost took me out," Kerri adds. "I've had many nights, where I'm lying in bed, staring at the ceiling trying to understand it all."

"Some things are not for us to understand," Ray interjects. "This I've learned for sure."

Kerri

"Cam, have you thought about rehab?" I ask, causing the room to go silent.

"Damn, why are you raining on the fun parade?" Cam quizzes. "Did you not hear anything of what I said? I don't need help because I'm not an addict."

"I heard you but with any addiction, most times the addict doesn't believe they have a problem. I know because I've been through that with Mike. But he decided to go to rehab. It was only supposed to be thirty days, but it's been almost three months."

"Gul, if you think I'm about to voluntarily sign my life away to some stranger, in a facility, in a different state; you've lost your mind. I'm proud of Michael but nah, I'll pass." Cam says.

"He was just like you, adamant about not needing help until he spiraled, too. He's had problems since he was a child, stemming from his mom abandoning him."

"I don't have those problems, Kerri, move on. I get that y'all are worried but I'm good and before you ask, Shelby, I'm not going to church."

"Sister, I don't know what inner fight you're having with self, but don't be too proud to get help." I reassure her.

"I agree," Shelby adds. "And Camille, you should know, prayer is what pulled you through. We've all been going to High Point Christian Center and Pastor Magnolia Reeves has prayed for you, on many occasions."

"Oh, speaking of High Point, I met with Todd's mom, Denise."

"Denise French?" Lyn questions.

"Yea."

"I met her, at the hospital. She's a chaplain at Methodist and I was really rude to her."

"Maybe you'll see her again, seeing she's excited for this baby."

"Really?"

"Yes. I went into the meeting with my wall up because I thought she was going to be on this, stay away from my son hoe, type stuff but she wasn't."

"Chloe," Ray laughs, "did you really think that woman was going to call you a hoe?"

She shrugs. "I didn't know what to expect. Todd told me about a woman, he was with, a few years ago who lied about being pregnant, so I expected her to hate me, just on principal. But surprisingly, she likes me and is excited about the baby."

"That's because she's an intercessor and has God's ear," Shelby says. "She'd know if you were lying."

"Well, all things considered, I'm happy for you Chloe. My only advice, be careful and don't move too fast with this."

"I have no plans, even though he's already proposed marriage."

"Chloe, please tell me you didn't say yes?" Shelby asked.

"Hell no. I just got out of a bad marriage and I am not about to jump into another one, baby or no baby,"

I answer.

"That's understandable. You just got rid of one loser, the last thing you need is to get attached to someone who runs away so easily," Ray interjects.

"I know, but the funny part is, it's not even about my divorce because God showed me all the warning signs with Chris, but I ignored them. The next time I get married, it's going to be with the man I plan to do forever with and who has his heart in God. I will not make the mistake of marrying a man because he knows how to make me feel good."

"Amen."

"Well, you're better off single, anyway, because all men lie and keep secrets," Lyn asserts, gulping her wine.

"K," Shelby states. "You've gotten quiet. Is everything okay?"

"Did I tell y'all Adrian is a Bishop?"

"What? Kerri, you been getting it on with a bishop. Does he speak in tongue when he cums?"

Cam asks, causing all of us to laugh.

"No, cow but yes, I found out when I went to church with Ms. D. I guess with everything going on, I forgot to tell y'all."

"How are things, between y'all, anyway?"

"We aren't fooling around anymore, and I decided not to work with him. He's cool people but if I want to give my marriage a chance, when Michael gets home, I have to cut ties with what tempted me, in the first place. Oh, and his wife."

"His wife? She hasn't done anything to you, has she?"

"No, nothing like that but I met his wife, at the church that night and she gave off weird vibes." I shudder. "She just gave me the creeps and although Adrian is cool, I don't need those problems. Shoot, after watching Lifetime, all kinds of thoughts go through my head whenever I encounter someone who irks my spirit."

"Amen, to that."

"For more great news," Shelby says. "Brian's

cancer is treatable. Right now, he's on medicine to try and shrink the tumor but he'll eventually have to have an invasive surgery, to remove the tumor and maybe radiation but he's going to be okay."

"Oh, thank God," I tell her. "I was so scared when he told me his diagnosis."

"Wait, what? When did he tell you?"

I bite the inside of my jaw and silently curse myself for letting that slip.

"Kerri, when did Brian tell you he was sick?"

"Let me explain, Shelby," I say.

"I'm all ears."

"Oh shit," Cam says sipping her wine.

"Brian came to me, some months back. It was the day he'd gotten the news from his doctor and he didn't know how to tell you."

"So, you knew this entire time and didn't say anything? You knew when we were in LA and I made the comment of him acting strange?"

"I begged him to tell you," I say with my eyes

getting misty.

"Why did he feel comfortable telling you in the first place?" Ray asks. "Is there something going on with you and Brian?"

The room is eerily silent.

Shelby

"Kerri, is there something going on with you and my husband?" I ask through clenched teeth.

"No, of course not. I'd never do you like that. We've been friends since—"

"Cut the bullshit," I scream getting up. "We all know how long we've been friends, but it still doesn't explain why my husband told you about him being sick and not me."

I look at her as she twists the napkin between her fingers.

"Brian and I knew each other before you met," Kerri says.

"Say more, please." Cam instigates.

"We met in junior high school. It was before they moved to Knoxville. We tried to stay in touch, but we were young, and it was long distance. That was the last time I ever saw him, until the two of you met and starting dating."

"If it was that innocent, why didn't you tell me when I introduced y'all?"

"Because it was nothing. I hadn't seen him in years, so it wasn't like there was something to tell. We were kids, Shelby."

"Did y'all sleep together?"

"Shelby, I'm sorry I didn't tell you, but I begged him to and he promised he would."

"You still didn't answer the question. Did you and my husband ever have sex?"

"One time, before he was your husband because again, we were fifteen."

"Wow," Shelby says.

"It's not a big deal. I knew him, years before you met. We went to school together and out on a few, childhood dates, that's it. The sex, between us, didn't really count because it was both of our first times."

"Kerri, you need to learn to shut up," Cam says.

"What?"

"You just told that woman, you took her

husband's virginity."

"WE WERE KIDS!"

"I'm going to ask you this and you'd better not lie. Has there been anything between you and my husband since?"

"No, God no, I'd never disrespect you or your marriage. Shelby, you've been a sister to me. You were there when my parents and grandmother died, you've been with me through everything. I wouldn't hurt you like that.

That day, when Brian showed up, I hadn't expected him to tell me that. I thought he was coming to, maybe, plan a surprise for you. After he confided in me, I begged him to go home and tell you."

"It's cool," I tell her.

"I'm sorry," Kerri says. "I should have told you about knowing him, but I didn't think it mattered seeing it had been so long."

"Kerri, I can't be mad at whatever happened between you and Brian, twenty years ago but I'm pissed because of what has happened now. Especially seeing that he thought enough of you, to tell you first, rather than his wife."

"I don't think he meant any harm, Shelby. He was scared."

"Stop taking up for him because he wasn't scared to tell you."

"That's not my fault," she says, matter-of-factly, "because I didn't ask him to tell me. He showed up at my place of business. It's not like anything like this has happened before. It was bad judgment. But you have to know, I'd never do anything to hurt you."

I go over and grab my wine glass.

"Are we cool?" she questions.

"That's yet to be seen."

"But—"

"Kerri, learn when to shut up." Cam tells her.

"Chloe, are you okay? You're looking weird." Ray asks.

"I don't know, I feel—I can't explain it," she says rubbing her stomach.

"Are you hurting? Should I call Dr. Lane?"

"No, maybe I'm overreacting."

"You can never overreact when it comes to the health of you and this baby."

"I know but I'm fine. I just feel funny."

"Funny how, Chloe?" Shelby asks.

"I can't explain it but let's get through tonight and if I don't feel better, in the morning, I'll call Dr. Lane."

"Are you sure, because this sleepover can—

"Ah," she cries.

"That's it. Let's go."

*****

We're waiting around for the doctor to come back with test results.

"Chloe, calm down," I tell her, standing next to the bed. "Dr. Lane said everything with the baby looks good."

"I know, but it still doesn't help my nerves," she

says as the doctor walks in. "Dr. Lane, is everything okay?"

"Chloe, I'm concerned about your blood pressure. Whenever you have numbers, this high, we have to worry about preëclampsia. Right now, you aren't showing any additional signs, other than the blood pressure but I'd like to keep you overnight, just to monitor you. I'll have the nurse draw some more blood, in a few hours and check your protein level."

"What happens if she begins showing signs of preeclampsia?" I ask.

"The only option to stop preeclampsia is to deliver the baby—"

"No, it's too early," Chloe cries.

"Chloe, we aren't there yet," Dr. Lane reassures her. "We will continue to treat your blood pressure and start you on steroids, for the baby, just in case. However, as long as your tests remain normal, that little one will stay right where it is."

"Thank you, Dr. Lane."

"It's not a problem. You take care and get some

rest. I'll be back in the morning."

"Chloe?" Todd says rushing in. "Are you okay?"

"I'm fine," she tells him.

"We're going to go so you and Todd can talk. We'll be back in the morning."

Chapter 9

Chloe

"Are you sure you're okay?"

"Yes Todd, Dr. Lane is just worried because my blood pressure is a little high. He's going to keep me overnight, to monitor me."

He lets out a sigh of relief before sitting beside the bed.

"You don't have to stay. I'll call you if anything changes."

"Chloe, I meant what I said about being here for you and this baby. I've already missed out on so much, please allow me to be here with you, now."

I nod.

"Can I get you anything?"

"No, I'm fine. Good thing I ate before coming here."

"I'll get you more food, if you're still hungry."

"Maybe later," I tell him laying my head back.

"While we have time, would you like to talk? You can tell me what you'd like to do on our first date."

"Are you serious about that?"

"Yes. How else am I going to get to know the mother of my child and my future wife?"

"Todd—"

"I know, the marriage thing scares you and I am not trying to push it on you, but I want a family Chloe."

"I get that, but I don't want you marrying me just because I'm pregnant. One useless marriage is all I have the energy for, in this life time and the next."

"That's not what I'm insinuating but I want to be a part of my child's life and not just on court ordered visitation."

"I get that but I'm not willing to sacrifice my happiness for the sake of having you in the home. Todd, I wasted three years, of my life, that I can't get back with a man who only loved my stability.

Don't get me wrong, I knew I had no business marrying him, but all my girls were married, and I was tired of being alone. I'll never make that mistake again. If I choose to get married again, it'll be because I've met the man who is mine and his love for me, will show in his eyes and in his actions."

"How do you know I'm not that man?"

"I don't know you. We had a one-night stand that produced this," I say rubbing my stomach.

"She is our blessing and no matter how she was conceived; I have to think it was a part of God's plan. Babies are a blessing."

"Yea, but God doesn't condone adultery. And how do you know it's a girl?"

"My mother," he smiles. "Chloe, I know how we began but I'm choosing to believe you were praying for a sign, from God and He gave it. Sure, it was unorthodox but how many other signs did you overlook?"

"That's true but—"

"There is no buts. How about this? We do like I suggested. We have three months to get to know each other. During this time, we date one another."

"What if you don't like the person I am?"

"Do you smoke or drink?"

"No to smoking and yes, the occasional cocktail or wine. What about you?"

"Same. Do you believe in God?"

"Of course not. I was raised strictly atheist by parents who forbade me from reading the bible and I've never set foot in a church. I thought I told you that."

"Oh wow," he says, rubbing his head. "Uh—"

"I'm just kidding. Yes, I am a believer of God."

"Whew," he laughs. "I didn't know how I could explain that to my mom. Lord, my heart started beating fast. Well, you know I'm a believer. Where do you see yourself, in a year?"

"Raising this baby, running my magazine, hanging with my girls, traveling and co-parenting with you. What about you?" I yawn.

"Parenting with you, running my second restaurant, here and hopefully, married to you."

He grabs my hand.

"Okay, last question and then I'll let you rest. Now, think carefully because this can be a deal breaker. Do you snore?"

I scrunch my nose. "Really Todd?"

"Look lady, I have to know who I'm laying next too."

"Who said you'll be lying next to me."

"Girl, you know you want all this." He says standing to rub his stomach and I burst into laughing.

His phone rings as the nurse comes in.

"This is my mom. I'll be right back."

"How are you feeling?" the nurse inquires.

"I feel fine, other than a slight headache. Is everything okay?"

"Your blood pressure is a little high, so Dr. Lane wants to run a few more tests. I'm going to get some blood and urine. I'm also going to put you on a catheter and a heart monitor for the baby because Dr. Lane doesn't want you getting up."

She explains the procedure, for the catheter and when she's done, I lay back and close my eyes as she puts on the monitor. When I hear the baby's heartbeat, I close my eyes.

"I'm done," the nurse says. "I'll be back later and if you need anything, press the call button."

"Thank you."

I look at the door and Todd still hasn't come back, so I turn out the light, over the bed and roll on my side.

"Be good, little one. You need a little more time."

Sometime later, I feel Todd get in the bed with me and I don't fight, when he wraps his arms around me.

"Dude, what the hell are you doing?"

I turn at the sound of Todd's voice to see Chris in bed with me.

"Chris, what the hell are you doing? Get up."

"The hospital called because I'm still listed as your emergency contact."

"Dude, I've been here over three hours."

"I was busy," he shrugs.

"And you thought bringing your ass in here, climbing into my bed was the best choice."

"Well, you always were sexy when you weren't talking."

"Chris, get the hell out of here and I'll be sure to update my paperwork."

"Is this your baby daddy?"

"Chris—ah," I cry out.

"Baby, what's wrong?" Todd asks running to me.

"My head, ah."

"Nurse! Nurse!"

Kerri

I make it home from the hospital. MJ is with Ms. D because we were supposed to spend the night at Chloe's house and the quietness is eerie. I go over to the alarm and it shows on stay.

"Hmm," I say putting the code in before grabbing my phone to open the app. I'm trying to see if I set the alarm incorrectly, when I left.

Turning back, "got damn it, Mike. You scared the crap out of me."

"I'm sorry, I didn't hear you come in."

"What are you doing here? I thought you weren't coming home until next week."

"I wanted to surprise you. I called Ms. D and she said you were spending the night at Chloe's."

"I was but she had to go to the hospital and they're keeping her overnight. How long have you been here?"

"For about an hour. Is Chloe okay?" he questions.

"She's pregnant and was having some pain but she'll be fine."

"Chloe's pregnant? Wow. I haven't talked to Chris in a while."

"They aren't together anymore."

"What? Are you serious? Man, I've missed out on a lot, these last six months."

"We all have," I tell him. "I'll have to fill you in later. On another note, you're looking good."

"I feel good," he replies. "Going into inpatient therapy was worth it. I only wish I'd gone earlier."

I go over and sit at the table and he joins me.

"I was telling Cam about that but, of course, she doesn't think she needs help."

"Spoken like a true addict but the crazy part about it, she's being truthful. Someone who has an addiction doesn't see what everybody else sees. Camille is looking at the world from the standpoint of, as long as I'm still who I am; then I'm fine. Reality is, she's spiraling and sometimes it takes hitting rock bottom, a few times to know, this isn't where you want to be or belong."

"Yea but I thought the overdose would have been an eye opener."

"It was, for y'all but not her because she isn't ready to deal with that. And the more y'all push her, the farther she'll go into her shell, with her addictions. The next time, she'll cover it better."

"I know and sometimes I wonder if the overdose was intentional," I tell him.

"She's the only one who can answer this but, where she is now, she'll never admit it."

"Did you ever think about suicide?"

"To be honest with you, yes. While I was tricking my mind into believing, as long as I drank, I wouldn't have to deal with my problem. However, I realized, those same problems will be there when I sobered up. So, yeah, I've thought about suicide, but I could never go through with it.

Nevertheless, some people have because they feel suicide is their only way out. And there's a misconception that suicide is easy but that's the farthest from the truth. Suicide is the hardest thing, for anybody, because to them it's their last option.

They've tried the talking, the therapy or the drugs and they've tried to be strong enough to pull themselves out but when you can't, and they no longer want to be a burden; they choose suicide. Others may not have tried to commit suicide but when you want the thoughts in your head to silence themselves, you will do just about anything."

I looked at him as the tears fall. "I didn't know it was that bad. How were you able to survive?"

"This is going to sound cliché, but it was only by the grace of God. One night, I'd gotten so drunk that I was in the alley of this bar, trying to use the bathroom. I don't know how I ended up there, but I was. When I finished and turned around, there was a gun in my face.

The dude, a young kid, wanted everything I had. At first, I didn't comprehend what was happening until he pressed that gun to the middle of my forehead. You talk about sobering up, quick. I'd foolishly left my wallet, keys and phone on the bar. He got so angry that he pulled the trigger, but it jammed. It was then, as my life was flashing before—" he stops when he gets emotional, "my life was flashing before my eyes that I saw you and MJ. God allowed me to feel the pain of what you'd feel, being notified of my murder. Kerri, that dude pulled that trigger, three more times and each time, the gun didn't shoot."

He gets up from the table.

"I knew I had to get back to y'all, so I made up my mind to do it and I did."

"Why didn't you tell me?"

"You would have offered me pity and I didn't need pity, I had to have a plan. The plan was rehab and getting my family back. Kerri, I went to rehab and now I'm back to fight for you."

He kneels beside the table. "Kerri Janeen Davis, will you marry me again?"

"First," I say, "there's something I have to tell you." I swallow hard. "I slept with Brian."

Ray

Since our night was canceled and Anthony has been asking to see me, I decided to meet him at the apartment. I made it before he did and it's evident, nobody has used it.

Between his traveling and everything that has been going on with the girls, it's been a few weeks since I've seen him, outside of work and my body is craving his touch.

I turn on the heat, kick off my shoes and lite a few candles but then I stop and sit on the side of the bed. A few minutes later, Anthony comes in.

"Hey, what's wrong?"

"I can't do this."

"Are you not feeling well?"

"No, I'm not feeling this. I'm sorry Anthony but I shouldn't have come here."

"Raylan, I love you," he says.

"Whoa," I say, standing up. "Anthony, don't go

there."

"What? It's true."

"No, it's not because this isn't love, this is, lust because we were both what each of us needed. Anthony, I'm not looking for another relationship, right now and neither should you be.

Both of us are going through huge transitions and moving on, so fast, wouldn't be fair to our children. Yes, I cannot lie and say I didn't enjoy being with you, but the fact remains, this is wrong. And as much as I hate to admit it, I'm yearning for your touch."

"Doesn't that tell you something?"

"Yeah, that I need to pray for strength to resist temptation and I need some new toys," I reply.

"Was I only a distraction for you?"

"Isn't that what I am, to you?"

He sighs.

"Anthony, we have to be honest with what this is. I slept with you because it'd been months since I had the affection of a husband who vowed to always love me. You slept with me because your house is stressful. This isn't love.

And jumping into another relationship, without taking the time to heal from a previous one, is a setup for failure. I don't want that. If I can be honest, I don't know if I ever want to be married again."

"I'm not talking about marriage, Raylan, I just enjoy the peace you bring. All Kris does is nag—"

"Stop," I tell him. "Don't bad mouth your wife to me because until the divorce is settled, she's still your wife. At some point, she was worthy of that title, don't speak less of her now."

"Damn, when did you become a fan of Kris?" he scoffs.

"I'm not but complaining about her, to someone you've cheated with, isn't the way to handle things."

I sit in a chair across from the bed, to put on my shoes.

"Anthony, you were an outlet for me, to get away from my troubles but had my life been good at home, I never would have cheated on my husband. And even now, if there was ever a chance our marriage could have been saved, I probably would have. However, that's not the case but if you have a chance with Kris, take it."

He shakes his head. "Nah, I'm done."

"Just don't let this," I say pointing between us, "be the reason you choose divorce without seeing if there's a solution to the issues with your wife. What we had was a temporary distraction from our problems and I now know this can never happen again. I only hope it hasn't ruined our working relationship because I love what I do."

"It hasn't but thank you."

"For?"

"Being honest. Raylan, you are a great woman and don't allow the troubles with Justin, to close your heart off from marriage, in the future because you'll make a real man, proud to have you. Who knows, maybe even me."

I smile. "Who knows but at this point, in my life, I

have to find peace and protect my now."

"Your now?"

"Yes, my present. I realize that I need to limit access to people and things, in order to protect my now; for the sake of me and my children. They are going through a tough time and I need to make sure, they heal properly in order to not harbor hate, in their heart, towards their dad.

I need that too, in order to be able to see love, if it shall present itself to me again. Anthony, I spent years with a man who didn't love me, and I will not go into another relationship without knowing, without a shadow of a doubt, that he loves me, but it'll be, on my time.

I can, honestly say, this thing between us, isn't love and neither is this what God has for me. Maybe I should have figured this out, before sleeping with you but, I couldn't help it. Anyway, and this is no way, meant to be offensive but, we're better as co-workers, not lovers."

He smiles and stands up, holding out his hand to

me. I take it and he pull me into a hug.

"I'll see you on Monday, Raylan."

"I'll see you Monday."

Getting home, I walk in to find Rashida on the couch and the boys stretched out on the floor.

"Hey, what are you doing home?"

"Chloe got sick and has to stay overnight in the hospital. She's going to be okay but that ended our girl's night. What are you watching?"

"It's a movie that Sis. Renee, from church, told us to watch. It's called The Grace Card."

"What's it about?" I ask, sitting next to her.

"A man loses his son and he's filled with anger and bitterness. He's a police officer so he gets paired with a man, named Sam, who is also a pastor."

"The dad is mad at the world but he's also mad at God but—"

"He's learning that life can change in an instant, but we have a chance to rebuild relationships by extending grace," Tristan says, finishing Rashida's sentence.

"Mom," JJ says sitting up. "I know we're all mad at daddy, but I think it's time we talked. I don't know how our relationship will look, going forward but he deserves grace too."

Before I can stop myself. I have tears pouring down my face.

Lyn

Sitting in the floor, of my still empty apartment, with my back against the wall; I play with the bottle of pills. The last time I went to the emergency room, the doctor gave me a prescription for pain.

At first, I didn't get them filled but my nightmares have gotten worse and they count as pain, don't they?

I twist off the childproof top and spread them, on the floor, in front of me; putting them in groups of two.

"We've been in a relationship," she corrects, "for over three years. It started off as sex and an occasional dinner but after six months, things evolved."

"But you knew he was married?"

"I did but he said you all were just together for Kelsey. Look, I am not here to stake my claim on him because he's already mine but, like I said, I am tired of his lies."

"Let me guess, he said we were going to get a divorce?"

She nods, yes.

"And you believed him, even though he comes home to me, we take family vacations and pictures— "

"He also comes home to me; we take family vacation and pictures too. Lyn, I know this is a lot to take in, but Paul said, he's only staying because you're unstable."

I smirk, "and you're here now because you've realized what, he's been lying? Kandis, there is nothing unstable about me."

"No? Then why were you contemplating suicide, a few months back."

"Then why were you contemplating suicide," I mock, recounting the pills. "Yea, why are you contemplating suicide Lyn? Huh? Are you unstable like Kandis thinks?" I say talking to myself.

"FUCK KANDIS!" I scream, throwing the empty bottle across the room. "I'm not unstable but I'm tired." I begin to rock back and forth. "God, I'm tired. Do you care?"

I laugh. "Of course not. God doesn't care about me. Why should He when I haven't cared about Him?"

I pick up two pills and pop them into my mouth. Opening the bottle of water, I swallow them.

"God doesn't care."

I hear music playing, next door.

"Every now and then, I remember when I went out on my own. Searching here and there for someone to care. Feeling so all alone but through the fire His love did not come to an end. In my weakness, your grace was greater than my sin. Over and over again."

I turn and hit on the wall.

"Can you turn that down! Hello! Turn that music down!" I scream, throwing the water bottle across the room.

"The moment came and went; I was feeling discontent. Where was I supposed to go? Then You came along, making right what once was wrong. Your love never failed and now I know."

I get up and look around to find something hard. I pick up a shoe and hit on the wall.

"Please turn that music off!"

"I made some foolish mistakes because I'm in sin, it drove me away. Each time I let myself down, your grace always abounds. And I wanna say thank You, for giving me another chance. You didn't throw me away."

"Please stop!" I scream, falling into the floor.

"I don't know where to start and I don't know where to begin. All I know was, every time I looked around, you keep on catching me."

I begin to cry, hitting the floor. When I see the pills, I crawl over to where they are, picking two more but then, I remember throwing the water.

The song, next door replays. I get up and go into the kitchen, putting the pills into my mouth. Turning on the water, in the sink, I cup my hand under it and sip the water.

I try to swallow but the pills will not go down. I get more water but still, the pills feel like they have tripled in size. I try more water but the same thing.

I spit them in the sink.

"What do you want from me?" I scream, sliding down into the floor.

More music plays.

"Show me your face, fill up this space. My world needs you right now. My world needs you right now. I can't escape, being afraid. Fill me with you right now. My world needs you right now"

"Please stop," I cry. "Please stop."

"Power fall down, bring with it a sound that points us to you right now. Erase substitutes right now, fix what I see and God please fix me. My world needs you right now. Let us see you right now."

I jump up and grab my purse, but it falls. When it hits the floor, the only thing that comes out is a card. I pick it up.

Chaplain Denise French.

Sitting in my truck, in some parking lot, I keep turning the card over in my hand. I finally let out a breath and dial the number.

"Hello, this is Denise French."

"Chaplain French, you may not remember me, but I need your help."

"Lynesha Williams," she cuts in. "I knew you'd call."

"How, how did you know?"

"You asked God a question, didn't you? My address is 9632 Pilgrim Way, Olive Branch, MS. I'll be waiting for you. 9632 Pilgrim Way, Olive Branch, MS;" she repeats before hanging up."

Shelby

I call Brian to tell him I'm on the way home, but he doesn't answer, which is scaring me. I send him a text and now, I'm speeding, praying there is no police anywhere around.

Parking in the garage, I hurry into the house, dropping my stuff next to the table in the hallway.

"Brian?" I call out, my heart beating fast. "Brian, where are you?"

There's a note taped to the wall. I take it and open it.

Shelby, I've loved you since meeting you that Saturday morning in Target. Sure, you had on leggings, an oversize tee and a head wrap but you were the finest thang, I'd ever seen. Who knew, all these years later, you'd still make my heart flutter. You've changed my entire world and I couldn't imagine doing life without you.

Now the fun part ...

Roses are red, violets are blue, to find the second clue, go to where there's a little person whose just as sweet as you.

I rush upstairs and into Brinae's nursery to find a picture of us, hanging across from her crib. I gasp. It's an oil painting of our first family photo. Then I notice another note, taped to her crib. I reach in and touch her, and she stirs but doesn't wake up.

A chair is still a chair, even when there's no one sitting there but a chair is not a house and a house is not a home; when there's no one there to hold you tight and no one there you can kiss goodnight.

You'll find the next clue, in the place where I will always kiss you goodnight.

I go into our bedroom and see a new picture hanging in the sitting area. It's an array of photos, from the time to first met, up to our tenth anniversary, from last year.

"Oh my God," I say as tears spill from my eyes. I look around the room until I see a blue pillow, on the couch. I go over and see that it's made from one of his shirts, I always wear.

I pick it up and see the note on the back.

I remember when loving you wasn't easy. It wasn't easy, baby but I stuck on in there with you and we made it. Sugar, we made it, through it all. Now let's keep it up, cause I ain't had enough. You and me, girl, go a long way back. Yeah, we go a long way back.

I then hear music coming from downstairs.

Luther Vandross.

Let me hold you tight, if only for one night. Let me keep you near, to ease away your fear. It would be so nice, if only for one night. I won't tell a soul, no one has to know. If you want to be totally discreet, I'll be at your side; if only for one night.

I turn the corner, to see him standing inside of a sandbox, filled with sand. There're drinks on the table and candles everywhere.

"Brian," I say through tears. "What is this?"

"I can't take you to the beach, right now so I decided to bring a little of the beach to you."

"How did you know I'd be home, when I was supposed to stay at Chloe's? Did Kerri call you?"

"Kerri?" he asks confused. "No. This was supposed to be a surprise, for when you came home tomorrow but when I got your text, I put everything into motion."

"Your eyes say things I never hear from you and my knees are shaking too but I'm willing to go thru. I must be crazy, standing in this place but I'm feeling no disgrace, for asking."

He holds out his hand.

"May I have this dance?"

I don't move.

"Let me hold you tight, if only for one night. Let me keep you near, to ease away your fear. It would be so nice, if only for one night."

"Shelby, what's wrong?"

"Why did you tell Kerri about being sick and not me?"

His hand falls to his side.

"Why was she the one you ran too?"

"Babe, I can explain," he says, shaking the dirt from his feet and coming over to me. "This entire process has been scary but when I finally got the results and they said cancer; I couldn't bring myself to tell you. It was almost like, I blamed myself for getting sick because you'd begged me to get the headaches checked."

"And?"

"I messed up. There's no if, ands or butts about it. I messed up. The thing is, I knew Kerri—"

"Before me," I finish. "Yea, I found that out too, but I can't be mad about that. What I'm pissed about, though, is the fact neither of you told me. Brian, I'm your wife and I should have been with you, through the test and doctor's visits. Yet, you left me out. The least you could have done was tell me when you got the results. Do you know how embarrassing it was, for her to say, she knew first, before me?"

The song changes to Luther Vandross', My Love.

"I didn't think, Shelby."

"There's only you in my life, the only thing that's right. My first love, you're every breath I take. You're every step I make."

"Can you please stop that music?" I scream.

He presses mute on the remote.

"I messed up Shelby and I'm sorry. I never meant to hurt you."

"What else is there?"

"What do you mean?" he questions.

"What other secrets are you keeping? Do I have to worry about being blindsided by anything else that my husband should have told me? Is there anything else you've confided to Kerri?"

"No, baby. I promise."

"Is there something going on between you and her?"

"No, God no."

"I wish I could believe you, but I don't."

"Baby, please wait," he says when I turn to leave.

"Brian, I appreciate the effort you put into this but right now, I'm not in the mood to sit in the midst of a sand box with you, after hugging this out and forgetting it, neither am I forgiving.

Especially knowing, one of my best friends is who you ran too when you were scared and not me." I state. "Oh, I also know that y'all took each other's virginity. Imagine how that must have been, to find out in front of all the girls. Good night Brian."

I go upstairs to undress and shower when I hear a loud crash. I run back down, to see Brian in the middle of the floor having a seizure.

"Oh my God," I yell, rushing to him. "Brian." I turn him on his side before getting up to get his phone off the mantle.

"911, what's your emergency?"

"My husband is having a seizure. The address is 1024 Galaxy Trail. Please hurry. Brian, baby, hold on."

Now Available .... The Finale

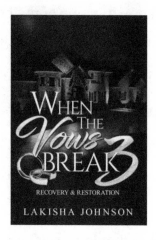

When the Vows Break 3: Recovery & Restoration

https://www.amazon.com/dp/B07WVFHCH6

As always, I could not have done this without your support. THANK YOU!

I pray you've enjoyed When the Vows Break 2 and you'll stick around to see how things end, for the six pack.

Well, for five of them because you know, Cam has her own series, Ms. Nice Nasty. This series isn't available yet but it will be re-released by the end of August.

If you've enjoyed, the series, so far, please review and share it, shout it out on social media and tag me.

I'd love to hear from you.

Happy Reading,

Lakisha

About the Author

 Lakisha Johnson, native Memphian and author of over fifteen titles was born to write. She'll tell you, "Writing didn't find me, it's was engraved in my spirit during creation." Along with being an author, she is an ordained minister, co-pastor, wife, mother and the product of a large family.

She is an blogger at kishasdailydevotional.com and social media poster where she utilizes her gifts to encourage others to tap into their God given talents. She won't claim to be the best at what she does nor does she have all the answers; she is simply grateful to be used by God.

Again, I thank you for taking the time to read my work! I cannot express what it means to me every time you support me! If this is your first time reading my work, please check out the many other books available by visiting my Amazon Page.

For upcoming contests and give-a-ways, I invite you to like my Facebook page, AuthorLakisha, follow my blog https://authorlakishajohnson.com/ or join my reading group Twins Write 2.

Or you can connect with me on Social Media.

Twitter: _kishajohnson | Instagram: kishajohnson | Snapchat: Authorlakisha

Email: authorlakisha@gmail.com

Also available

Broken

Gwendolyn was 13 when her dad shattered her heart, leaving her broken. Her mother told her, a daddy can break a girl's heart before any man has a chance and she was right.

Through many failed relationships and giving herself to any man who showed interest, she knew she had to get herself together. So, she gave up on men.

Until Jacque. He came into her life with promises to love, honor and cherish her; forsaking all others until death do they part. Twelve years later, he has made good on his promises until he didn't.

https://www.amazon.com/dp/B07QZCW9ZX

The Family that Lies:

Forsaken by Grayce, Saved by Merci

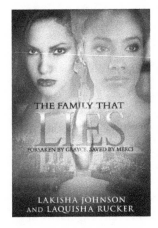

Born only months apart, Merci and Grayce Alexander were as close as sisters could get. With a father who thought the world of them, life was good. Until one day everything changed.

While Grayce got love and attention, Merci got all the hell, forcing her to leave home. She never looks back, putting the past behind her until ... her sister shows up over a decade later begging for help, bringing all of the forgotten past with her. Merci wasn't the least bit prepared for what was about to happen next.

Merci realizes, she's been a part of something much bigger than she'd ever imagined. Yea, every family has their secrets, hidden truths and ties but Merci had no idea she'd been born into the family that lies.

https://www.amazon.com/dp/B01MAZD49X

The Family that Lies: Merci Restored

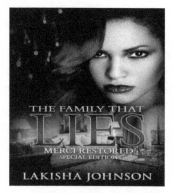

In The Family that Lies: Merci Restored, we revisit the Alexanders to see how life has treated them. Three years ago, Merci realized she'd been a part of something much bigger than she ever could have imagined. Sure, every family has their secrets, hidden truths and ties but Merci had no idea she'd been born into the family that lies ... without caring who it hurts!

Now, years later, Merci finds herself in the midst of grief, a new baby and marriage while still learning how to pick up the broken pieces of her life.

All while Melvin is still raising hell!

In this special edition of The Family that Lies, there will be questions answered and new drama but I have to warn you ... there will also be tragedy, hurt and of course LIES!

https://www.amazon.com/dp/B07P6LGQQ6

The Pastor's Admin

DISCLAIMER This is Christian FICTION which includes some sex scenes and language. ***

Daphne 'Dee' Gary used to love being an admin ... until Joseph Thornton. She has been his administrative assistant for ten years and each year, she has to decide whether it will be his secrets or her sanity. And the choice is beginning to take a toil.

Joseph is the founder and pastor of Assembly of God Christian Center and he is, hell, there are so many words Daphne can use to describe him but none are good. He does things without thinking of the consequence because he knows Dee will be there to bail him out. Truth is, she has too because ... it's her job, right? A job she has been questioning lately.

Daphne knows life can be hard and flesh will sometimes win but when she has to choose between HIS SECRETS or HER SANITY, this time, will she remain The Pastor's Admin?

https://www.amazon.com/dp/B07B9V4981

The Marriage Bed

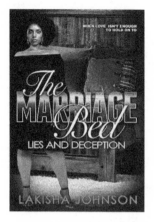

Lynn and Jerome Watson have been together since meeting in the halls of Booker T. Washington High School, in 1993. Twenty-five years, a house, business and three children later they are on the heels of their 18th wedding anniversary and Lynn's 40th birthday. Her only request ... a night of fun, at home, with her husband and maybe a few toys.

Lynn thinks their marriage bed is suffering and wants to spice it up. Jerome, on the other hand, thinks Lynn is overreacting. His thoughts, if it ain't broke, don't break it trying to fix it. Then something happens that shakes up the Watson household and secrets are revealed but the biggest secret, Jerome has and his lips are sealed.

Bible says in Hebrews 13:4, "Let marriage be held in honor among all, and let the marriage bed be undefiled, for God will judge the sexually immoral and adulterous." But what happens when life starts throwing daggers, lies, turns and twists?

https://www.amazon.com/dp/B07H51VS45

Still Fighting: My sister's fight with Trigeminal Neuralgia

What would you do if you woke up one morning with pain doctors couldn't diagnose, medicine couldn't minimize, sleep couldn't stop and kept getting worse?

What would you do if this pain took everything from your ability to eat, sleep, wash your face, brush your teeth, feel the wind, enjoy the outdoors or even work? What would you do if this pain even tried to take your life but couldn't shake your faith?

Still Fighting is an inside look into my sister's continued fight with Trigeminal Neuralgia, a condition known as the Suicide Disease because of the lives it has taken. In this book, I take you on a journey of recognition, route and restoration from my point of view; a sister who would stop at nothing to help her twin sister/best friend fight to live.

It is my prayer you will be blessed by my sister's will to fight and survive.

https://www.amazon.com/dp/B07MJHF6NL

The Forgotten Wife

All Rylee wants is her husband's attention.

She used to be the apple of Todd's eye but no matter what she did, lately, he was just too busy to notice her.

She could not help but wonder why.

Then one day, an unexpected email, subject line: Forgotten Wife and little did she know, it was about to play a major part in her life.

They say first comes love then comes ... a kidnapping, attacks, lies and affairs. Someone is out for blood but who, what, when and why?

Secrets are revealed and Rylee fears for her life, when all she ever wanted was not to be The Forgotten Wife.

https://www.amazon.com/gp/product/B07DRQ8NPR

Other Available Titles

When the Vows Break 1

A Compilation of Christian Stories: Box Set

Dear God: Hear My Prayer

2:32 AM: Losing My Faith in God

Bible Chicks: Book 2

Doses of Devotion

You Only Live Once: Youth Devotional

HERoine Addict – Women's Journal

Be A Fighter - Journal

CPSIA information can be obtained
at www.ICGtesting.com
Printed in the USA
LVHW111708171019
634537LV00004B/608/P